GEOFF WARR was born in 1951. After spending an idyllic childhood in West Yorkshire, at the age of nine he moved with his family to Surrey. There, his experience of grammar school was fraught and academically unproductive. It was followed by a four-year gap during which he worked intermittently on building sites, in factories and as a refuse collector in order to finance extensive trips to Europe, the Middle East and the overland hippy trail from Turkey to India.

At the age of 22, Geoff, who was by then married, enrolled as a mature student at the University of Leeds, where he graduated with a B.Ed. in 1977. His first job as a teacher was at a residential children's centre in County Durham. For the following 35 years he worked as a teacher, manager, principal, staff trainer and consultant at a variety of social work and special educational needs establishments. At the heart of this work with troubled teenagers was the challenge of trying to understand the fragmented stories of what had been going on in their lives and, if possible, nudge their narratives in a more positive direction.

From the beginning of his career, Geoff was inspired by the idea that someone should write a book about this subject matter, and about the fact that there are times when the kids and staff can be not only touched but transformed by their mutual encounters.

Alright Now is Geoff's debut novel, and the first of the Jack Warren stories which tell these tales.

Alright Now

Geoff Warr

SilverWood

Published in 2021 by SilverWood Books

SilverWood Books Ltd
14 Small Street, Bristol, BS1 1DE, United Kingdom
www.silverwoodbooks.co.uk

ISBN 978-1-80042-093-9 (paperback)
ISBN 978-1-80042-094-6 (ebook)

British Library Cataloguing in Publication Data
A CIP catalogue record for this book is
available from the British Library

Page design and typesetting by SilverWood Books

ALRIGHT NOW

Preface

Little Flo

We went to see Dr M. again this morning. I've been before, with Daddy, a few times, but today, Mummy came too.

Daddy used to be frightened about seeing Dr M. But I said to him, out loud, "Don't you be a scaredy cat. I'm not anymore, and now I don't even have to make myself be brave, 'cos seeing Dr M. is as cosy as a pair of warm pyjamas. First of all, she has this lovely smell, just like Granma. And second of all, she's got more toys than anyone in the whole world. She's got this tiny sandpit, and a big bowl with water and things to pour out of and into. And best of all, she's got loads of toy animals and all sorts of different dolls. That's what I like to play with. The dolls. I've got one that's me, and there's one that's Daddy, and one for Nancy (who used to be my sister). And then there's one for Mummy (which really should have brown coloured skin, but doesn't, so we just have to pretend). And at last, there's one for Dr M. so she can watch what we do and hear what we all say.

Really, Dr M. doesn't join in properly. She just lets me play. Sometimes she asks a question if she doesn't understand, but mostly she's still and quiet as a mouse.

Today, the three of them let me play by myself while they talked to each other. I think it was a lot about the new baby, which will come out soon. I tried my hardest to listen, but I couldn't hear properly. Or understand. Apart from one thing that Mummy said to Dr M. Actually, she said it twice. It was about me. She said, "I used to feel sick with worry about Little Flo, but now that's gone. I know she's going to be fine. It's going to be alright now. I just know it. It's going to be alright now".

1

It's just after three on a gorgeously warm and sunny late September afternoon. We had thought, during last week's savage storms, that summer was completely over, that colder and darker were all we'd get from now till the spring. But today arrived like a surprising and welcome guest. And then Charley came round, half-an-hour ago, brought a little package, rolled a joint and departed in a haze of purple smoke and a shuddering blast of the Floyd pouring out of the Volvo's open windows.

Little Flo is upstairs, having a rare afternoon nap. Fizz is singing in the kitchen, where she's baking brownies for the raging munchies which are bound to hit us in another hour or two. I'm gazing at the Chevin, with its tree-lined sides turning to gold and rocky outcrops gleaming in their most delightful way, and I'm soaking up the sunshine with all my might, and wondering whether to put on Mozart, or make tea, or roll another joint.

Just as I decide on doing all three, Fizz appears. She's holding *The Times Ed*. It's open on a jobs vacant page. She's pointing with what looks like serious determination at a large boxed advert. It says, in big-lettered bold type "ARE YOU EXCEPTIONAL?" She says, "I thought you might like to look at this." She means, "You'd better." I take the paper, and read with a cool innocence, and complete ignorance. And I am, immediately, there and then, hooked, lined and sinkered.

The fates have conspired.

God help us, and God bless us, every one.

Little Flo has been making snuffling and gurgling noises which are drifting downstairs. As I go into her room, she is sitting in a nest of cushions and pillows, clasping Ted to her cheek, holding out her other hand in a please pick me up now gesture. I'm still holding *The Times Ed*, which I tuck under my chin, lifting her up two-handed and then hoisting her onto my hip. "Come on Flo, let's go downstairs. We've got work to do. We're on a mission." She does her hooking on like a limpet routine, and gives the gurgle which means, "Let's go." We bounce down the stairs and park ourselves on the front step, having picked up a bean bag for Flo and planted her on it, wedged between me and the door frame. Marley comes to investigate, sniffs, wags her tail and joins us. I look again at the advert – slowly and carefully reading each word out loud, searching for their intent, scheming my response.

ARE YOU EXCEPTIONAL?

Do you have the skills, patience, resilience and determination to work with some of the most troubled and troublesome young people in the country? If you believe that you are able to make a positive contribution to this uniquely challenging environment, please get in touch. Completed application forms, with accompanying personal statements, must be submitted by October 15th, 1978.

"So Flo, what do you think? Do you reckon your Daddy is exceptional? Do you think that I've got any skills? Would you and Mummy say I'm patient? Marley, your assessment of my resilience please."

Then I say to the pair of them, "Speaking on my own behalf, and in my own favour, I wish to cite the following: The write-up in the *Otley Gazette* after last week's resounding defeat against Harrogate, describes me as 'an indefatigable lock-forward', so I wish to claim that as a tick in the determination facing adversity box. And yes, I do have a bunch of skills, a capacity for patience, a core of determination and a first name familiarity with troubled and troublesome, which in combination may mean that perhaps I could make a half-way viable candidate. But, to get to the nub, and therein the possible rub of it, let me add to their list another category. Desperate. 'Cos the ugly truth is, if I don't manage to get a job soon, we could accurately describe our situation as being halfway between dire and desperate. So, I reckon that I'll just have to be perfect for this job. Whatever it is. I'm going to ring, right now, for an application form, and I'm going to write them a scintillating and irresistible personal statement, just as soon as I've rolled another joint."

The problem with the personal statement wasn't the writing of it in the first place. Once we'd had tea and were halfway through that second joint, I had a great surge, and out it poured in a mighty venting, a crescendo rising from mere statement to extravagant rant. In the cooler light of the following morning, I looked again at the eruption. I ditched three-quarters, turned down the ambient volume by half, expunged the most florid metaphors, and contented myself with:

To whom it may concern,

I am submitting this personal statement in response to your advertisement in The Times Ed *of September 30th. You pose the question, "Are you exceptional?" I offer you the following, in the hope that you will concur with my self-assessment – that I am – and then conclude that it would meet our mutual best interests to invite me to an interview at your establishment. My basic contention is that I have a number of personal characteristics, attributes, talents, interests and abilities, each of which is unusual. They combine, I believe, to create a composite character who is, frankly, unique, and would be, I believe, well suited to work in the environment you describe.*

To start with matters physical and external. My appearance is uncommon. Even from a significant distance. More so on closer inspection. I stand over a foot taller than most men. I have the largest hands I've ever seen on any human. I have one-and-a-half deep brown eyes, and half a bright green one. I have one relatively small and elegant ear, and one hugely inflamed and upset-looking cauliflower. I have a calm, confident and reassuring basic disposition, and usually deport myself as a genteel giant. This normal demeanour is, however, transformed into its polar opposite in two contexts – rugby and water polo-sports for which I have an extravagantly wild enthusiasm.

I believe that I have developed an affinity with the type of young people you describe as being "troubled and troublesome." This arises in part, I think, from the fact that my own adolescence was disrupted, and prone to sporadic explosions – which themselves led to me being subjected, usually seething and snarling, to various forms of psychological intervention. I thereby gained not so much an interest in, as an obsession for learning about theories of the mind, which I felt I needed as equipment for basic self-defence. Most of my personal recollection of counsellors, therapists, doctors and psychiatrists is that they combined to create (in my own obsessively considered opinion) stunning examples of what not to do and how not to do it. Thankfully, there was one amongst that galaxy of professionals, one who broke the mould, and offered me a lifeline.

Following various teenage psychological skirmishes, and expulsion from grammar school, I had the privilege of enjoying a six-year sabbatical from the bastions of the British learning machine, and the challenges of mental health interventions. I undertook various unskilled jobs, travelled widely, and spent extended periods living on a kibbutz and an ashram.

I made the choice, at the age of twenty-four, to enrol as a mature student on a teacher-training course. I had, by then, taken to the notion that I would make a good teacher, although the prospect of a mainstream school setting did seem slightly dull. Whilst at college, all of my teaching practice settings were of the inner-city, deprived variety. I encountered kids who were disengaged, hostile and seriously stroppy. I felt able to not just cope but thrive in such settings.

I have little notion of the precise circumstances which lead to young people being placed in your establishment. But I do have personal experience of that sense of being uncomfortable, ill-at-ease and angry, suffering inside my own skin and railing against everyone and everything in my environment. I am someone who knows about being in a mess, and I know how it feels to be teetering, at times gleefully, on the brink of disasters. I have some opinions about what has helped, and what has hindered my development. I have a belief in my own painfully polished capacity to provide positive support to kids who are messed up and whose lives therefore wreak havoc.

And I am at this point in my life both available for work and in desperate need of a job. I therefore plead that you invite me for an interview, where I hope I can convince you that I am worth employing.

14

Yours sincerely,
Jack Warren.

I read it all to Little Flo, knowing that she would neither judge nor comment. Marley gave me, and the letter, a cursory sniff, but showed no real interest. But then, the question, should I show it to Fizz? Bit risky. I could get told off. Told to tone it down. Might have to do more editing and be made to write a proper one. Dangerous. So. Quick. Stuff it into an envelope, lick it, stick it, stamp it, run to the post box, drop it in.

Done.

Into thine hand, O Mr Postman, I commend my future employment prospects.

As I walked back into the house, Marley gave an exasperated sigh, which Little Flo copied. I put one in the back-pack, the other on the lead, took Fizz by the hand, and we all went off to walk up to the top of the Chevin.

It took us almost an hour, about par for this particular course. We sat on our rock – fortunately vacant – and indeed had the whole area pretty much to ourselves. Muffled sounds of others in the half-distance hovered on the brink of earshot. Marley did a bit of snuffling and sussing out in our immediate vicinity, seemed to judge it kosher, and then came to sit with us, scenting the breeze and admiring the view.

From our rock, you can see all of our terrace, and just about make out the dormer window of Little Flo's bedroom. Our cultivated-flower-and-veg patch stands out clearly, neatly distinct from the wild and weedy mess which surrounds it. You can see Otley Rugby Club, scruffy outbuildings, pavilion, stand, pitch and posts. In fact, the whole town is neatly laid out, and snugly nestled into its bit of the Wharf Valley. And there's a huge, though definitely not endless vista of woods, rich fields, dry stone walls and moors up top. For me, it is the most perfect piece of Planet Earth. And it's home. Home again, here and now. Just as it used to be home when I was a kid, when I was one quarter of a family which was whole, where everything used to fit, naturally, together, safe beyond doubt or question.

Fizz takes in the view with a steady gaze. We're looking out together, not at each other, and without breath or blink, she asks, "Did you send off that personal statement yet?"

I tell her, "Yes, indeed I did. Sealed the envelope before I could read it again. Dropped it in the box just before we came out."

"You didn't want me to see it?" she asks, with a bit of an edge in her tone.

I say, "Yes, I did want you to see it, but I couldn't manage to do show and share. I was worried that you might have made helpful suggestions. And then I would either have wanted to win any argument of 'who's right' or accept the loss of the argument, which would then mean changing stuff, and I just wanted to get it off my hands and put my balls in their court. "

I take a short pause, to think and breathe, then say,

"But now it's gone, I'm happy to tell you what I wrote."

Immediately, and surprisingly kindly, she says, "Go on then. Tell."

I say, "I told them that I've got one-and-a-half brown eyes and half a green one, and one cauliflower ear, and that I used to be considered crazy, but that now, I'm neither a complete vegetable nor an absolute fruit cake."

She snorts with sufficient gusto to attract Marley's attention, and says, "That makes you sound absolutely irresistible."

And I say, "I'm afraid I just might be."

And Fizz gives me one of her long "mmms".

Then we share a weighty pause. Followed by Fizz saying, "They're bound to say yes. Or at least invite you to an interview. And unless you do mad ranting at them, they'll give you the job. In fact, they've probably got loads of vacant posts that they can't manage to fill. Everyone says that those places are forever struggling to get hold of staff, let alone keep them!"

I ask "Does Catch 22 apply to aspiring job-seekers, or only to demented post-holders? Do you think there's a perfect pitch of being just mad enough to work there?"

Fizz says, "I don't know. We'll see."

Then, after a big fat beast of a pause, she says "If you do get a job there, we'll have to move, you know. Have you thought that through? Do you think you can handle that one?"

I don't say anything in reply, but just look out at the view. It feels like it's our home. Home to the bone. And then I feel the massive solid rock that we're all sitting on start to dissolve, like a sugar lump dropped in hot tea. I get a hint of that taste on the back of my tongue. But it's not sweet tea. It's that sharp, metallic, sulphurous taste, the one that comes with crazy.

Three days later, the letter comes inviting me for an interview.

2

By the end of that week, everyone seems to know. Everyone we know knows. And loads of people that we don't even know seem to know as well.

Thursday morning. Wild, windy, promising wet. Marley and I pop into town, leaving the girls tucked-up indoors. We're on a mini-mission. To the newsagents for a pouch of tobacco, packet of skins and the *Guardian* – who needs *The Times Ed* now? To the butcher's for tonight's chops, and to the offy for bottles of Newcastle Brown. As we walk into the newsagent's, we bump into Chris, fellow marauding forward from the rugby club.

He's still sporting the remnant of a spectacular black eye from last week's match against Gosforth. He says: "So, Jack, you've got the interview then? When do you think you'll be jumping our little ship, you miserable rat?"

I say "Chris, I dunno. I really don't know what the job is, or what the pay is, or what the place is, or anything about the set-up. I suppose I'll get a better picture when I go for the interview. It's next Tuesday morning."

Old George, behind the counter, has a pricked ear and an aroused interest. He's already got my *Guardian*, Old Holborn and Rizlas in his hand, and is following our chat with a professional gossip's concern.

"Here, Jack lad," he says. "Is it Beecliffe, the name of that place you're off to?"

"Yeah, that's it."

"Well," he says, "You'll be able to learn all about it on telly, this Wednesday. There's going to be an hour-long documentary. I saw the trailer last night. They're doing a whole series, like 'Britain's most dangerous kids' or summat. Looks bloody grim!"

In the butcher's, while Jan is wrapping up my chops, she gives me a bit of a knowing nod, and raises one eyebrow above the rim line of her glasses.

"Have you seen, Jack? It's going to be on the telly next week, that place you're off to."

"Yep, George has just told me."

She muses quietly for a moment, then says, "Ah, bless 'em. Poor little mites. Though there was one of 'em on the trailer. Not a little mite that one. He looked like a young version of that boxer

19

Joe Bugner, only not quite so pretty." After another brief pause for thought, Jan says, "Oh well, I suppose you know what you're doing."

I assure her that I certainly do not know what I am doing, and that nothing's settled yet, and we'll just have to wait and see.

She warmly wishes me "Good luck, love."

I thank her.

In the off licence, I ask for three bottles of Brown, then change my mind to four. And the bottles come with the foreboding comment, "Aye, Jack lad. You'll probably be needing 'em all."

Marley and I walk back home. But she's the only one wagging her tail.

On Tuesday morning, I get up quietly, by myself, leaving the girls snoring gently and sleeping peacefully. In the kitchen, Marley greets me by opening one eye, giving a couple of desultory twitches of the tail, sighing deeply and returning to her slumber. My tea and Weetabix are swallowed in a rather forlorn silence. As I'm staring at a smudge of jam on the table, a bit of last night's dream floats into mind. The Joe Bugner look-alike's got hold of Little Flo. She seems OK but Marley is definitely not. Raised hackles, growly snarl. Fizz is trying to take Little Flo, but Joe holds on tight, and keeps shouting, "Get that black bitch away from me," and I'm looking in from the back yard, unable to move or speak.

I pour the rest of my tea down the sink, and go off to catch the bus. The journey into Leeds takes forty minutes. Mercifully, I've got the *Guardian* and wrap myself up in the glowing report of Leeds United's away win over Liverpool last night. Bremner was out injured, but Giles apparently played a commanding midfield blinder, and Sniffer Clarke scored one and made one, and Norman Hunter Esq. was only booked the once for his leg-biting misdemeanours. So, with United rampant, plus a gratifying completion of the crossword, I arrive at the station feeling, for that moment, positively perky.

Leeds to Darlington, via York, with a bit of a wait, takes a couple of hours. The day is dull, the colours subdued, my mood drifts to somewhere between resignation and a vaguely worried apathy. Gradually, I realise that I'm not actually thinking about the interview or the job at all. But I am fretting over the prospective turmoil of leaving Otley.

Again.

I was eight years old the first time.

I remember us all getting into the car. The removal vans have just left. The neighbours are waving us goodbye. And I'm staring out of the car window, doing this funny breathing, a sort of mix between sighing and panting. And Ma says, "Are you all right, Jack? What is it? What's wrong?" And I say "Nothing," because I don't know how to and I don't want to try to explain to her that I just have to completely fill myself up with Otley air before we head into the great unknown of a new life in Surrey.

There and then, in that car, I had no choice, no options, had no escape. Now, on this train I do. I can, if I want to, go straight back to Leeds from York. I can go home, tell the girls, "Decided against it." I can arm myself with this week's *Times Ed*.

I can hold out until I get something, anything, local. And, more or less as soon as I realise that I don't have to go through with it, I start to get curious, wondering what Beecliffe might be holding up its mysterious sleeves.

The last bit of the journey, from Darlington to Beecliffe, is by bus. Half-an-hour's worth. I ask the conductor to let me know when I get to the stop. He says, "You'll know alright. Bloody great sign. Plus you can see the scaffolding and the cranes for the new unit from miles away!"

I look out of the window. Mostly it's dull and drab, with empty fields, scruffy bits of hedge and occasional sheep. I'm playing with the lump of dope I've got in my pocket. It's wrapped in a bit of tin foil. It's the size of a baked bean. It's enough for a couple of big fat joints for the way home. Quite suddenly, and out of the blue, I get a powerful rush of paranoia. The brain voice says, "This place is some kind of prison for kids, right? Maybe they search everyone who goes in. Maybe they've got sniffer dogs. Maybe I'll achieve the double of staying jobless and getting busted all in one go."

I get off at my stop, cross the dual carriageway, then furtively bend down at the foot of one of the posts holding up the bloody great sign, and stash the dope.

As I'm walking along the driveway, following the pointer signs to reception, I begin to wonder if, as well as sniffer dogs, they might also have security cameras everywhere, and has anyone clocked my little manoeuvre?

I get to reception, relieved and unscathed, tell them who I am, receive a welcoming smile and the offer of a cuppa, which I accept, taste, and immediately regret.

It's a quarter of an hour before the designated interview kick-off time. I can't focus on the newspaper, most of which I've read anyway. There isn't room for me to do pacing up and down. I recognise that this is the same kind of stomach-churning that I get before a real match kick-off. But, this time, there's no prospect of a cathartic release through an almighty physical dust-up.

Time stutters along.

Mind manages to anticipate some prospective questions, but baulks at any answers – apart from dull or dumb ones. "Are you exceptional?" "Yes. Right now I'm a candidate for the exceptional tongue-tied brainless stuttering fuck-wit of the year award."

My kindly coffee dispenser from reception answers the internal phone, says, "Yes, OK then." She catches my eye. "Mr Warren. They're ready for you now. Would you like to go through?"

I walk into a large office. There's a big desk, cleared of everything apart from a pile of application forms. Behind the desk, two of them. Both sitting, neither gets up. One of them invites me to sit on the single chair, in front of the desk, lower than them. I'm much too big for the chair, which feels like it's been borrowed from an infants' school.

One of them talks. He says that the interview will last for about half an hour, and that I will have the opportunity to ask any questions I may have at the end of it. He gives me their names. Ken Kaminsky, Head of Assessment, and Dr Michael Aveyleigh, Principal of Beecliffe. I immediately forget which one is which. He says, "We'll start with your personal statement, address some of the issues which arise from it, then move on to the requirements of our work, and your potential to become a member of staff here. OK?"

I respond with a noise which I intend as a warm and confident affirmation. It comes out as a semi-strangled croak. I try to finesse this into a preparatory clearing of the throat, but this turns into a brief but intense coughing fit. A small quantity of glistening phlegm is expectorated in the process which, after a short airborne moment, attaches itself to the back of my left hand. I give it a rueful glance, then plunge my hand deep inside my trouser pocket.

And now, with a second and successful throat-clearing "Aahem," I am ready.

I do have some recollection of their questions. But I remember virtually nothing about my answers. One of the inquisitors, Ken Kaminsky as it later transpired, was actually quite warm and friendly. He started by saying that he had, to his surprise, enjoyed reading my personal statement, and had found it interesting. I appreciated this ego-endearing flattery, and felt a twinge of emotional engagement.

But, as for the other one. Oh, deary me. The fact that he's a Doctor of Psych. triggered all my defence systems. I wanted to outsmart and outmanoeuvre him, rather than open up. His questions about my personal experiences in the world of shrinks had all the comfort and reassuring warmth of a three-foot cattle probe. I smelt hostile innuendo on his breath. I thought him clever, and sly, and shifty. And I thought, "I know you, you bastard. You're the one who wears the white coat 'cos you have to prove to yourself that you're on the right side of the sanity line. You won't allow a hint of self-doubt anywhere near you, will you? You arrogant twat."

And, he has this slight trace of a foreign accent. I can't quite place it. His vowels sound like cultured English. But "th" is the giveaway. He can't quite get his tongue to the right bit of his teeth.

There is just one chunk of the whole interview which I do remember, clearly and completely. Dr Aveyleigh had been pontificating about patterns and characteristics of maladaptive behaviour. He asked my opinion about the ontology of aggression in boys who themselves have been bullied or otherwise abused. I spouted something about identification with the aggressor, but added that, in my view, "adolescent male aggressive behaviour is, despite some cultural variation, a virtually universal phenomenon. It is, I believe, one of *the* characteristic traits" (which I pronounced like mates or hates) "of the male teenager." And he said, "Here, Mr Warren, you have made an error. In English, wid de word trait, we do not pronounce de last T."

I smiled, and thanked him with all the grace I could muster, through the grimace of my clenched teet.

At the end of the half hour, they had, presumably, elicited what they needed. Then Mr Kaminsky said, "OK, Mr Warren, your turn now."

I paused, for what I considered to be a finely considered moment, before saying, "Thank you. For now, there is nothing I wish to ask." I stood up to leave. Neither offered me his hand. I therefore bowed, presenting the crown of my head to them, in the manner of the samurai warrior.

I left the room, the building and the whole estate, without a backward glance. I marched with single-minded purpose to the bloody great sign, retrieved my stash, crossed the road, sat down alone in the bus shelter, and rolled a big fat joint. As I was about three-quarters of the way through it, a mum approached hand-in-hand with a toddler. Fearful of undercover secret police, I walked away, re-crossed the road and waited for my return bus to Darlington. I was thinking about "de T" and started coming up with more and more clever and cutting ripostes, which I was performing through a range of accents and an array of attitudes and gestures. The kid at the bus stop opposite watched, and pointed, and started to laugh, along with her mum. I took a flamboyant bow. Then my bus arrived, same driver and conductor.

Off home.

When I finally walked back into the house, it was just gone ten o'clock. I'd popped into the Junction, initially intending to have a swift half, which somehow turned into a not quite so quick three pints, then diverted into The Golden Plaice for a battered sausage and bag of chips.

At home, in the lounge, Fizz is lying stretched out on the sofa, crossword in hand, soft jazz on the stereo. She opens her arms for a long hug and neck-nuzzle, then says, "So. Tell all. How was it? How are you doing?"

I tell her, "It was mixed. It was all right. I'm OK, I think. I'm not sure. I do know that I am absolutely knackered."

She interlocks he fingers, raises arms above her head, and yawns.

"Mm. Me too! Knackered, to a pulp. Little Flo was stressed and flustered. Heavy going. I think she's been tuned in to your nervy brain waves for most of the day. Poor thing."

She yawns again. Longer and deeper, a harbinger of the last gasp. I say, "Shall we call it a night for today then? I will tell all, but in the morning."

Fizz says that'll do fine. She gives me a light cheek peck, a brief butt grope, and is gone. I check on Flo, who does cosy murmuring as I tuck her in, then slides back into warm and welcome sleep. I go back downstairs, select Santana, plug in the earphones, roll up the remainder of the bean-sized bit, and lie there, with Marley at my feet, relishing the moment, and wishing that life itself had a pause button, which I could find, and press, to hold it all, just there.

I wake up two hours later, crick in the neck, busting for a pee. I shuffle off, do the bits, then climb into bed with Fizz, where we lie like spoons and sleep like happy pups.

3

Charley came round at ten past eight. Little Flo and I were waiting for him, she in my arms. He took her from me, gave her a big kiss and a long hug, and asked both of us if he should take her off to bed. I said sure. Flo gave her 'mmm' affirmative, so off they both went.

Flo's habitual response to anyone apart from me or Fizz, is one of nervous suspicion – and frequent antagonism. She seems to be so frightened of, or so hostile to strangers that they freeze on the spot, look alarmed, and look to us for the "what do I do now?" cue. But not so with Charley. Right from their first encounter, four years ago, when she'd just had her third birthday. He'd introduced himself, called her Little Princess, and seemed oblivious to any possibility other than them becoming immediate best friends. And so they have been, ever since. Flo always senses Charley's imminent arrival – usually about ten minutes before he gets here. She has this specific and absolutely steady smile to say he's nearly here. She had it this time, which was why we were awaiting his arrival together.

Various scraps of noise float downstairs. There was a gradual diminuendo, ending with a quiet Little Flo, and a two-toned hum coming from Charley. Another couple of minutes, then deep, calm, peaceful silence.

Charley walks into the lounge, joining me and Fizz. He says, "Job done. Fiver please."

I say, "Thanks Charley. Worth every penny. Put it on the bill."

It's quarter to nine, Charley says he's got something unusual. We both say, in harmony "What'cha got?" and Charley beams and tells us, "Tai sticks! Just got them this afternoon from Mad Andy. Haven't sampled any yet. He told me it's best not to drive on this stuff, on account of the hallucinations which tend to be distracting, and the floods of tears that come with the giggling fits, which are blinding. So, whaddya think? Shall we? Can I stay the night?"

Fizz says, "If you think you could leave here without us mugging you for your sticks, then you crazy."

And I say, "Beecliffe's going to be on the box in five minutes. Can we watch that straight and then get wrecked?"

29

It's agreed. Sound plan.

We settle down, each with a nice cup of tea and a packet of ginger nuts to share.

The opening shot of the documentary pans around what looks like an absolute idyll of English village life. A dozen white-painted semis surround a patch of green, in the middle of which there's a substantial tree with a long knotted rope hanging almost to the ground. Neighbouring hedges, bushes and shrubs are all decked out in fresh new leaf. Bees buzz round blossoms. Birds twitter. High cotton-wool clouds sail across a spring-cleaned sky. A bright and cheerful sun shines down.

The narrator, a woman, says, "For the past 35 years, Beecliffe has been working with some of the most difficult, dangerous and destructive adolescents in England. They are sent here from an area spanning the Midlands to the Scottish borders. This centre, the largest of its type in Europe, is about to open a new unit, providing a maximum security facility, designed to be escape-proof. The new unit will be home to its adolescent inmates for periods estimated to range from eighteen months to several years. It is divided into three distinct "houses", through which the inmates are required to graduate in order to achieve any prospect of gaining their freedom rather than incarceration in the adult prison system. The 'Sequential Treatment System' operated in the unit is the brainchild of Dr Michael Aveyleigh, Beecliffe's recently appointed principal. Most of the adolescents coming into the unit will have been tried, and found guilty, of offences including murder, rape and arson. Others will be deemed to have such serious behavioural problems that they pose a grave danger to themselves and/or others. During the following programme, we will be talking to Dr Aveyleigh about his plans for, and his concerns about, this project. We will meet some of the staff who work at Beecliffe, and we will try to get a feel for what it's like to be here from the inmate's point of view. Some of what you are about to see is genuinely shocking. None of it, we believe, is sensationalised. All of it is true."

Charley says, "How long does this go on for?"

Fizz tells him it's an hour. He says, "OK then. I'll just roll one now so it's ready for after."

The camera seems to have lost interest in the quaint village-green scene. It takes us about a hundred yards along a gently curved road. We turn left at the sign which proclaims "Beecliffe Regional Assessment Centre." There's an L-shaped building with three separate entrances. The whole thing is big. Red brick, moss and lichen-covered tiled roof. Metal windows, white painted, quite recently done, slightly threadbare. No litter, no graffiti. The sun is still shining, but not so brightly as it did over in the quaint village, which we are now told comprises on-site staff accommodation. But this is where the kids live during their initial assessment period.

We're told, by the narrator, that the assessment process should take six weeks, but sometimes kids get stuck there for much longer. We're also informed that occasionally, kids come back for re-assessment, and that these are known by the staff as "returned empties."

Having revealed the physical layout, the camera focuses

onto one of the doors, which opens. A man emerges, short and stout in stature, close cropped hair, looks army. He begins to walk down the path which leads to the dining room. No backward glance. He's followed by a single file crocodile of kids. They're all wearing identical blue parkas, the ones with orange linings and hoods with a bit of mock fur around the edge. About half of the kids have the hoods up. For those whose faces are exposed, the camera does the blur effect. Most walk with downcast gaze. One of them seems to clock the camera. He gives the finger.

Cut to the office of Dr Michael Aveyleigh. The narrator becomes the interviewer, but remains unseen. She says, "Dr Aveyleigh, since your appointment as Principal eighteen months ago, you have seen the building of the new secure unit reach near-completion, you have appointed more than twenty additional members of staff, and you have introduced what you describe as a revolutionary process of assessment and treatment. Tell me about these dramatic developments."

At this point, Charley lights the joint, takes a couple of enthusiastic drags, holds his breath, passes it to me with excited gesturing of smoke, pass, don't waste. We play the game of having to hold your breath till you get the joint back. It works until Fizz dissolves in paroxysms of coughing, which reminds me of my cough and flying phlegm incident at the interview, so I recount the tale with gusto, and before the joint gets down to the roach, we're all lying on the carpet, howling, at which point Marley joins in the vocals, so we don't quite catch every syllable and scintilla coming from the Good Doctor. Our eyes are crossed, and we pay no heed to de T's.

The remainder of the programme continues despite us having degenerated into a most disrespectful and inattentive audience. I am transformed into a finger-pointing heckler, arguing the toss with the Doc every time his face appears on the screen. Fizz is keenly interested in the shots revealing the staff accommodation, but is unable to hear anything much of the story-line above the din that Charley and I are making.

There are various bits which certainly deserve our undivided attention. There's a scene with Ken Kaminsky. He's having a chat with a girl who has just been physically hauled away from another kid. The two of them had come to messy blows, blood spillage looked imminent. Ken's saying something along the lines of, "Listen Bev, I know you're upset about getting involved in another fight, but this is only the third time you've been restrained all week. When you first came here, it was more than that every day. You ARE making progress." Bev looks unconvinced. She says, "Just fuck off and leave me alone." And to his great credit, Mr Kaminsky doesn't retaliate, or force the point. There's a kind concern about him, which looks genuine, and comes through the camera lens and the TV screen. He's powerful enough to calm our shenanigans for a few minutes, but then the Doc re-appears. So for me, it's back to shouting mayhem.

When it gets to the second advert break, Charley asks if we've got any booze in. We haven't. So he volunteers to nip to the offy, before it closes. While he's out, the programme resumes. A kid is being interviewed. Not a poor little mite. A big one. It's the young Joe Bugner look alike. It's his third time round the Beecliffe block. He's a re-returned empty. After his last assessment, he was allocated to a training school (an Approved School in old money) in Yorkshire. Whilst there, he allegedly assaulted five other kids and three members of staff, breaking and dislocating a number of bones in the process. Then he allegedly tried to burn down a dormitory full of some kids who had annoyed him. No deaths, but lots of damage. That's why he's back again. This time the assessment is to take place under lock and key. He's a candidate for the new secure unit.

Hello Joe.

4

I suppose it was writing the personal statement which started me thinking about it all again. That stuff about most of the shrink world being prime examples of what not to, and how not to. Recognising that, for me, one of them was entirely different. And that, with me, she had made all the difference. I honestly believe if it wasn't for her, I could still be there now, clocking up my first decade, locked into a permanent battle. Diagnosed as being possessed by a rock-solid, official madness.

My journey into the nut-house had kicked-off with a spectacular sequence. First, the assault. Then being sectioned under the Mental Health Act. Then being placed in the secure ward of the Adolescent Assessment Unit. Then the initial hearing, then remanded back for the detailed forensic psychiatric reports.

By the first time I met Dr M, I'd probably done a whole month of complete silence. I simply hadn't said a word to anyone. Not since I'd repeatedly tried to punch, kick and bite the policeman who was arresting me. I'd managed to get a mouthful of his arm. He'd been trying to get an armful of my neck. I'd got the powerful impression that he was trying to strangle me. I'd managed to get my chin inside his forearm. That allowed me to breathe again. Managed to prise and roll his arm an inch, which enabled me to get a decent mouthful, so I attempted the mighty munch. Then he let go all right. I suppose he made a quick reassessment, concluded that he couldn't safely complete the arrest single-handed, so he used his truncheon. Knocked me out, cold.

Once I was conscious again, I had the urge and the opportunity for sore reflection. And I thought that, after having had a bit of policeman *in* the mouth, I was not going to let anything *out* of the mouth. Not a word. Too dangerous. I didn't even say "No comment" when prompted. The whole business, from being arrested, then interviewed, then charged, was for me a weird silent movie – though everyone else had speaking parts. And once the Juvenile Court had remanded me back to the Adolescent Unit for the "extended and detailed assessment" of my mental state, I just stayed schtum. The silence became a habit. Various mind inspectors kept seeing me. Often in pairs, they asked questions. A lot of obvious ones. Like: "Do you know your name?" "Do you know why you are here?" "Do you understand that you have committed a serious assault on a police officer?"

They also kept asking some strange stuff, about who's the prime minister? What year is it? What letter follows C in the alphabet?

I mean, really!

From my point of view, most of their questions seemed quite innocuous. I could've answered them without any serious risk or danger. But I didn't. I'd made a rule for myself, and I was sticking to it.

Actually, all of the questioning business didn't bother me that much. What did get me seriously, dangerously angry was, once they'd gone through their listed questions, plus any supplementaries that might have sprung to their minds, then they'd start talking between themselves, about me, as if I wasn't there. They'd have these conversations in which one of the White Coats would say something like, "Having now observed him closely on a number of occasions, to me, this does not appear to be a case of catatonic withdrawal – not text-book anyway. His physiological reactions seem to be essentially unimpaired." To which the other Coat replies, "I agree, my view is that his silence is quite consciously self-imposed, and, I imagine, self-controlled. We have no evidence suggestive of a delusional condition, and my hunch is that the most recent traumas have precipitated this current state." White Coat One chips in, "Basically, we still lack evidence for a confident diagnosis, so my suggestion is that we continue to administer the Largactyl at the current dosage – just to be on the safe side."

This kind of stuff is repeated for days. The Coats seem to be getting increasingly frustrated, and they don't appear bothered about revealing their irritation to me. I start to wonder whether or not they've moved on to intentional provocation, trying to goad me into a reaction. The between-themselves-in-front-of-me talk increases, as does their reference to, and use of, a variety of tentative diagnostic labels.

Then yesterday morning, mid-session, the thought just popped into my head. It arrived too quickly for me. I didn't have time to modify or censor it. So I laughed out loud. Howled, in fact.

I'd finally realised, and I delighted myself with my penetrating insight. They are getting wound-up, simply because they can't put Jack-in-a-box.

The next day was the first time I met her. The way I remember, it was absolutely instantaneous. Right from that very first moment, she looked, and indeed she smelt, completely different from the rest of them. For her, no white coat. She wore an ordinary-looking black linen skirt, blue cotton shirt, paler blue sleeveless sweater. Straight, light brown, recently-washed-looking hair. Bit of lipstick. No stethoscope, no plastic name-badge, nothing uniform. And, no smell of antiseptic hand-wash. Instead, a slight whiff of something nice, which reminded me of my Ma in a best outfit on a special occasion.

She has a clipboard, with an A4 size notepad, blank, secured to it, and a silver Parker pen. I'm delivered to her office by two of the ward staff. She comes towards me, having been sitting behind her desk. She holds out her hand, saying, "Hello, Jack. I'm Carol Mandrake. I'm the Senior Consultant for the adolescent ward, I'm pleased to meet you."

As soon as she holds out her hand, I take it in a kind of automatic couldn't-help-myself grasp, and keep hold of it for the couple of seconds her introduction lasts. Her hand is warm and soft and dry, and feels safe and soothing. My own hands feel huge, awkward, clammy, but she certainly doesn't flinch. It's me who lets go first.

She thanks the ward staff for bringing me, and asks them to come back in half-an-hour. They go off, quietly closing the door behind them. In front of her big and serious-looking desk, there are four low, comfy chairs around an even lower coffee-table. It's got a large potted plant in the middle, one of those with thick, pink, hairy stems, and leaves which are patterned in deep mauve and light green. It looks healthy and taken care of.

She says, "Shall we sit down here?" and takes one of the chairs, not waiting for me to reply or move. So, I sit down on the next but one. There's three feet of space between us. We both stay quiet, maybe for half a minute, but this quiet doesn't feel so tense and agitated as it does with the White Coats. She just looks as if she's ready any time, and capable of handling whatever I might say. I feel tempted – almost wavering on the brink of speech. But no, I keep schtum.

We sit some more.

Then she comes out with, "Jack, let me offer you something to think about. It's a quotation, from a psychiatrist called Dr Wilfred

Bion. I'm not sure if I've got it word-perfect, but I am confident that I know the sense of it. Here it is, "Lies act as poison to the mind. The truth is its food."

I started looking at her when she said she wanted to offer me something. Her gaze was averted at that point, but when she actually gives me the quotation our eyes meet and hold for a moment. Then she looks away, as if to give me time whilst the words sink in.

After a couple of minutes, she asks me if I like the quotation. I nod a couple of times and say, "Mmm." I'm close to thanking her, but don't. Don't want to rush it. Nor does she, rush it, or risk it. I'm able to sit, feeling safe and calm, for the first time in ages. It seems to me like she has this endless supply of quiet peacefulness, and she's offering to share it with me.

Several more minutes pass by, then she looks at me directly and raises her eyebrows in an unspoken invitation, a kind of wordless "Shall I?" So I return affirming raised eyebrows, adding a nod. And she immediately replies with, "OK then, let's give it a go."

After a long, deep and considered breath, she begins:

"Those two registrars. The ones who were with you yesterday. They've spoken to me. They said it was extraordinary. They said that after all this time of you saying nothing, remaining absolutely silent, giving nothing away, that suddenly, for no apparent reason, you just laughed out loud. A big, booming belly-laugh. They said they were shocked – completely taken by surprise. Said they didn't know what to make of it."

She leaves me time and space, to take it in, consider what she's said, and think about whether or not I want to reply. I choose not to, but it's a close call.

We sit, quiet.

Later, she says, "The half-hour is nearly up now, Jack."

I respond with a nod.

She says, "I'd like to see you again tomorrow, here in my office. Would you like to see me?"

Again, I reply with a mute nod. She smiles, and says, "Good, I'm pleased."

Soon after, there's a light knock on the door. It makes me jump, and my stomach gives a quiet but powerful shudder. She talks through the door, "Just one moment, we'll come out together." And from the corridor, a voice replies, "OK, we'll wait here till you're ready."

I clear my throat. Somehow, she knows I'm about to say something, so she offers me her full attention, and she waits. Time too stops and waits. Then I say, "Jack-in-a-box!" and she says "Aah," with encouraging interest. And we both laugh, just a little bit, together.

I went to see her again the next morning, and the one after that, every morning, in fact, Monday to Friday, for the next six weeks. From ten o'clock until ten to eleven. We always sat in the same two chairs we'd used on the first morning.

Once the silence had been broken, the floodgates gradually opened up, and out it all poured. Towards the end, I was telling her just about everything, without that feeling of having to weigh it up first, or needing to explain or excuse or justify, or spice things up or tone them down.

Once I'd said, "Jack-in-a-box", and we'd laughed together,

I'd felt convinced that she would automatically understand anything and everything I could possibly say to her, but she was both clever and kind enough to prevent me from wrapping her up in some cloak of imagined magical powers. She said, from the start of our session on day two, "Jack, we both have to take the truth very seriously. I'll make you a promise, right here and now, that I will always do my very best to be honest with you. This means that, whatever I say to you will be, to the best of my knowledge and understanding, true. So, if it's a fact, for instance that today is Wednesday December 12th, 1966 and it's three minutes past ten, then I'll state that as a fact which I know to be true.

"Here's another true fact. I have to write an Assessment Report about you, which will go to the court, to help them decide on the consequences to you – for having resisted arrest and injured a police officer. I promise that I will truly tell you what I've written in the report, and why."

We share a medium-size pause. Then.

"It's also true, Jack, that at the moment, there's lots of stuff about you that I really do not know. I honestly don't know why you became silent for several weeks. I don't know why you broke your silence with me yesterday. I certainly don't know why your first words, were 'Jack-in-a–box', but I do feel that those particular words have some special meaning for you." She pauses, to give me the chance to say or ask something. I remain quiet, but will her to continue. She does.

"So, if I'm absolutely dead sure about something, that's what I'll say. And when I'm unsure, or unclear, about something,

42

I'll ask you to help to clear things up so that I can be more sure. And sometimes, if I've got a hunch about something, I'll share it with you, so we can both check it out. So, that's it. Here and now, I give you my solemn promise that I'll never tell you a lie or give you any bullshit. Does that sound OK to you, Jack?"

I nod.

Then she says, "Good, right. Now then, how about you? Will you promise to be as honest as you can? Will you promise that you'll only say stuff to me if you believe it to be true, whether it's stuff about facts, or beliefs, or feelings. Will you make that promise, Jack?"

I clear my throat. Then say, loud and strong, "Yep, I promise, no bullshit."

And she says, "Great."

After some more time has passed, she continues, "Now, Jack, let me add some more detailed information. We will be working together for the next six weeks. There will be an end-product to our work – a report which I will write and submit to the court. You know this fact already, so let me describe the context. The court will consider the content, and the recommendations of my report, and will ultimately decide on what should happen next. To you. Whether you should stay here longer, or be placed in some other type of institution, or placed on probation, or sent home. The court will make a judgement, about what you did, why you did it, and how likely it is that you may do something similar in the future. My job is to try my best to ensure that the judgement made by the court is based on an understanding of your case which is as complete and accurate as it can possibly be.

All of which means that you and I have a lot of hard work ahead of us. We DO NOT have a choice about the fact that this report and its recommendations must be completed, on time. But we do have quite a bit of choice about how we do this work. And a big element within that choice is about which direction we go in. Let me try to explain what I mean.

"For example, three weeks ago, you were involved in an incident which culminated in you being arrested. So, we could take the arrest as the starting point, and keep working backwards, step by step, until we reach something we could recognise as 'the thing which started it all off.' Or we could do the opposite. We could accept it as a fact that you ended up getting arrested, and we can try to figure out what the starting point might have been, and then we can work through how we think one thing actually led to the next.

"In fact, there's a third option too. We can just talk, and think about whatever you've got on your mind during any session. When we're working that way, things can come out jumbled, and will often feel confusing, but at least we'd know that the stuff which does come up is whatever is most on, or in your mind at that time."

She asks me to think about these different ways of working, and I say that I will try to. Then, Dr M gives me one of her straight, no bullshit looks, and says, "OK, do you have any questions for me at the moment? Or is there anything you want to say to me now?"

I say, "Mmm", and realise that I've got a whole head full of stuff, all kinds of different bits, jostling and pushing and shoving each other, fighting for the right to speak first. It's like one of those turnstiles you get at football grounds, that only allow one person through at a time, but I've got an unruly mob of a dozen at my gate. It's a wild and messy scrum. No nice manners, no 'after you's'. No-one gets through, and from me, no questions. No real comments. Only a brief 'Mmm'. Which, to my surprise, she seems to accept with warmth. Then, she replies with a 'Mmm' of her own, on a slightly rising intonation. And in the end, she delivers a long closing 'Mmm', full of hopeful encouragement, which makes me smile, and then she replies with a grin, which reveals a shiny gold tooth, upper-left, next to the incisor.

As I'm being taken back to the ward, I've already started looking forward to seeing her again the next day.

But, oh boy, oh boy, that night, my mind was jumping around like a pack of electrified rats in a hot metal cage. Thoughts and ideas, images and feelings were bumping into and bouncing off each other in a pantingly fast and furious mayhem, making me feel dizzy and sea-sick, and hurting the insides of my skull.

Dinner, as usual, was served at five. I was given, as usual, the choice between eating with the others or taking a tray in my room. Unusually for me, I opted not only for silence but also for solitude.

All the staff on our ward knew that I wasn't exactly a chatterbox, but they'd also sussed out that if they gave me simple choices between clear alternatives, I'd let them know what I wanted. So, when Marcus came later to collect my tray, he said, "Do you want to join the rest of us now, or would you rather stay here?" He gave enough of a pause after 'join the rest of us' to decline, and then a big enough gap to affirm 'stay here'. And then he just said, "Cool. You can still join us later if you change your mind." And I said, "Sure." He looked surprised, and, I think, pleased to have got a word out of me. He gave a nod before leaving, closing my door softly behind him. Really, I had the best part of three hours, in there by myself, no distraction, my head clanging with discordant clatter. It was like being inside a seriously crazy cinema, where I was sitting, surrounded by loads of screens, each one showing a different cartoon, some playing in slow motion, some playing in reverse time, some freezing the action at crucial, mostly nasty moments.

And the sound tracks were muddled.

It all felt harsh, loud, and jarring, like a fingernail scraping down a blackboard.

All this chaos was going on around me, and, at the same time, I was inside each separate bit. I had no option to look away, or to close my ears to the din.

The action sequences, and their accompanying dialogue, were too confused for me to keep up with. A lot of the scenes were familiar, recognised as a shifting mosaic of memories. But they kept distorting, jumping from bits of genuine recollection into fantasy, peppered with what ifs and if onlys.

As well as the chaotic moving pictures, I also had a bunch of still shots. These were totally different. Each one was crystal clear.

All of them were as solid as marble.

Every single one of them had become an indelible memory, built to last a lifetime.

There's the shot of Dad's coffin in the crematorium chapel. A single wreath on top. Parked in front of the curtains, on the conveyor. All set to move through to the fiery furnace. Waiting to take him from here to eternity.

The next shot is the one of my Ma's face. Frozen in a moment of stunned surprise, standing there at my bedroom door, one foot, one hand already in, clasping my wrapped and bowed present, catching the sight of a mostly-obscured birthday boy and a full back view of Nicky, naked, straddling me.

Then finally there's the big, banner headline from the *Staines and Egham Observer*, proclaiming "Gruesome Death of Local Teenager", and posing the question, in slightly smaller print, "Was this a tragic accident or suicide?"

That was it, the main triptych, around which all the other mad cavorting's swirled. I lay there on my bed, powerless to turn off the movie machine. A captive audience. Aghast and exhausted.

Just after eight-thirty, Marcus returned with my evening medication, a large shot of Largactyl.

I had never felt happier to see him, or more eager to embrace the blanket of oblivion which quickly ensued.

5

I didn't go into Otley myself until a few days after the TV programme. Fizz got more of the initial reaction from the locals than I did. Her summarised version was a mixture, ranging from, "Very admirable to go and work with those kids. I couldn't. I'd end up killing 'em," to, "You'd have to be bloody bonkers, or a saint, or both," to, "It's a good job Jack's built like a brick shit-house."

Apparently, in addition to the scene with the two girls having a minor bust-up, there was also some footage of big strong lads being held, not very well, by staff, plus Dr Aveyleigh reeling off stats about how difficult and dangerous these kids are for those working closely with them. He'd also spoken, evidently at length about the emotional costs incurred in this line of business, paid by the staff themselves, and by their families. All of which had gone well over my Tai-sticked-and-stoned head.

At rugby training on Thursday night, the boys gave me a more or less uninterrupted flow of piss-taking, plus a few lurid suggestions, but, then, a sudden and absolute re-focussing on to the much more serious business of Saturday's game against Fylde. A certain Mr Bill Beaumont was due to be playing. And I was due to be jumping against him in the line-out. So, quite naturally, Beecliffe shrank to insignificance.

That game had been an almighty challenge in anticipation and an extended nightmare on the day. We were stuffed, 47 points to 5. In the end Beaumont didn't play, but his stand-in, whoever it was, outclassed, outsmarted and outfought me in every aspect of play. At the final whistle, he gave me a pat on my dropping shoulder, ruffled my hair and told me that I could have real potential if I started to take my rugby more seriously. I didn't say it was my last game for Otley.

Sunday was for licking wounds, soaking in a Radox and mustard bath and staring, blank-eyed and brainless at the box.

On Tuesday, we were busy packing, because on Monday, the letter had come, offering me the position of houseparent on one of the Assessment Units. The letter also said that, along with the job, I'd get rent-free accommodation – which turned out to be one of those nice-looking semis by the green. It also urged me to take up the post as soon as possible.

On Thursday, the house contents were all inside the van. Charley came round, to take Fizz and Flo in his Volvo. Marley and I went with the blokes in the van. And that was it.

All of a sudden.

Gone.

6

I've got absolutely no clear memories of the first time I met Nicky. We were in the same class together at St James primary school in Englefield Green. I'd started there in January 1960 straight after our move down from Otley that Christmas. My first few weeks at St. James are a blur of feeling uncomfortable, awkward and self-conscious. I was homesick, lost and lonely, and on the few occasions I tried to say anything to anyone there, I was met with a reaction of gleeful gloating at my funny accent.

I suppose my novelty started to wear thin after a while, and awkwardness resolved into acceptance and the beginnings of friendships, with some of the boys, anyway. Not the girls though. Gender apartheid bisected the classroom. Playgrounds also had enforced separation. But we could look at each other, the boys and girls. And any chance I could get, or make, I would look at Nicky. Mute and moonstruck.

As soon as my eyes had lifted up from my blinding self-consciousness, as soon as I'd been able to scan the horizon, I'd seen her and she then became the only thing I wanted to look at. But I don't think I ever said a word to her, not at school. No, the talking didn't start until three years after we'd all left St James for our respective secondary schools, when we bumped into each other at the youth club. Not that I did much talking then – more mumbling and blushing really. At that time she was Kevin's girl-friend, and his bragging rights trophy. Kevin and I had become mates on a canoeing and sailing weekend at Thames Young Mariners, a couple of months previously. In fact, it was the water sports that got me to join the youth club. That, and the absolute certainty, in the world according to Kevin, which guaranteed us easy access to a whole bunch of girls, all of whom were evidently mad keen to be with boys just like us. So, the prospect was irresistible.

The reality, on that Friday night, came as a bit of a shock, which nearly put me off the whole business of the Engleteens Youth Club in particular, and girls in general.

The youth club was about four hundred yards from home, three-quarters of the length of Bagshot Road. I'd arranged to meet Kevin at the gate at 7.30ish. I arrived on time. He didn't. I hung around feeling big and uncomfortable, not sure what to do with my hands. Other kids started turning up, in twos or threes, plus the odd gaggle. I was on vague nodding terms with some, but felt reluctant to try any chat.

Then I saw him. But not just him, them, though I only recognised Kevin at first. He was always easy to spot. Strangely bouncy kind of walk, lots of extravagant throwing back of the head, loud laughter, and a fantastic mop of dead straight and absolutely blond hair, which he was forever tossing and twirling.

With him, in fact holding his hand, was someone who seemed quite familiar, but who looked altogether different. She was wearing a navy-blue reefer jacket, double breasted, lapels – what Ma calls a "bum-freezer". Beneath the jacket, there was a very thin flash of bright red miniskirt. Then a pair of long, smooth and shapely legs encased in honey-coloured stockings. Black shoes with a bit of heel. She wasn't just holding Kevin's hand. She also seemed to be hanging on to his every word and gesture. Oozing attraction. Demonstrating the most definite "I am with him" you could imagine.

Kevin called out "Wotcha" to me from ten yards. They both came close. Kev said, "Nicky, this is Jack." She said, "I know. I recognised his hands from half a mile away." Now, I really didn't know what to do with them, so I shoved one in the back pocket of my jeans, and use the other to scratch my head, ear and neck.

Kevin asked how we know each other. Nicky paused to see if I wanted to talk, waited, then jumped in herself to fill the gap, "From primary school. Jack arrived in the January when we were in Mr Gimlett's class. He looked several sizes too big for us lot. We all thought he must have been at least thirteen, and had been sent to our class 'cos he was too thick to cope in his own age group. We used to have this game of trying to make him say things, with his funny accent, so we could laugh at him."

This piece of information came as revelatory news to me. So, not just casual callousness, but a planned and organised game of taking the piss out of the big lump of northern oaf. No wonder I lost my Yorkshire accent so quickly.

Anyway, Nicky seemed to be amused with her reminiscences of school cruelties, which made me feel both scared of, and vulnerable with her. But these were minor considerations. The besotted puppy devotion of three years earlier had been re-kindled, and in fact burst into consuming flames, a furnace of hopeless adoration, fuelled by the tidal wave of growing boy's hormones.

And that was pretty well it, for then. Introduction and audience over. Their regal procession had to move on, for the admiration and delectation of all the other teenage mortals in the Youth Club. So, with two haughty hair-flicks from Kevin, and a half-twirl from Nicky, in they went, to drink orange Fanta and listen to The Beatles, crying out HELP.

I mumbled under my breath to their retreating backs, "I'm just so delighted to see you again, Nicky", in a tone which I hoped would convey sarcasm and a twist of irony. But in fact, the words were the plain truth, which I contrived to deliver wrapped in a slightly posh accent, scrubbed clean of northern hues, stripped bare of sincerity.

After that, I went more or less straight home. Told Ma that the youth club was a bit boring, that I hardly knew anyone, and didn't think I'd bother going again – why would I want to waste any time there?

But in fact, I did keep going. Most weeks. Got to know, and started to get on with some of the other kids, although they all felt vaguely irrelevant to me. I went because of Nicky. And, because Kevin had said that he now had his eye on Sarah, and that he would dump Nicky as soon as he got off with Sarah, and that I could have Nicky then to myself. And it all seemed very uncomplicated. As long as Sarah wanted to go out with Kevin, I would get Nicky, 'cos she wouldn't want the shame of being dumped and then being boyfriendless. I thought, she'll have to like me, she won't have a choice.

We certainly did get together, me and Nicky, eventually, but not according to that original, simple script.

I think that there were lots of factors which played their part in my transformation from being the butt of their jokes, to being – if not the centre of attention – then at least a fairly popular member of the gang. My erstwhile odd and separate accent had gone. My unusual size enabled me to buy cigarettes and alcohol in pubs and off-licences. Size and strength were also an invaluable asset whenever there were prospects of bother between our gang and anyone else's. Match- and race-winning skills in rugby and rowing were priceless. And perhaps best of all, a talent for making a bunch of people laugh, sometimes through cruel nastiness, more often through finding and revelling in the bizarre, and romping through the furthest reaches of the ridiculous.

And now, looking back on that all-too-brief period, it feels as if it was just about normal. Life, being lived in a day-by-day set of routines and commonplace ups and downs. Right up until 3.55 pm, on Saturday, March 19th, 1965, when the bolt exploded out of the blue. Nobody saw it coming. No preparatory "what-would-we-do-if" thoughts or conversations.

No. The reality came as the sheer shock of the previously undreamed-of.

A coronary thrombosis. And despite his heroic attempts at resuscitation, my big brother's valiant efforts to use his Boy Scouts first aid all proved useless.

The ambulance came, collected and delivered my Dad's mortal remains to the hospital.

D.O.A.

Not that I was even there. I'd been away at Thames Mariners for another water-sports weekend. Brother came to tell me first thing on the Sunday morning. He looked rough. Didn't say much. Just, "Dad's dead." And then someone was trying to make me drink sickly sweet tea. I couldn't swallow. Couldn't see. Think. Breathe. Bear it.

And that was that. The full extent of my knowledge. Dad's dead. Heart attack.

It took me years to ask about the facts and details of what had happened, and to realise why, previously, asking for this information had been such a dumb-struck impossibility.

My reality in the there-and-then was narrow, and flat, and dull. It had been a bright but freezing weekend. An uninterrupted deep blue sky, and an unrelenting mean easterly wind, that tore straight through life-jackets and anoraks, and made wet hands a source of pure agony.

We'd been in the canoes, practising the basics – straight ahead, sideways, backwards and then as soon as we started showing any rudiments of skill, we were into relay racing. Then it got to be fun, and hands at last got warm.

So, that's what we'd been doing on Saturday, and it was more of the same on Sunday morning. In fact, I was just getting ready to do my first leg of a relay, when I noticed the little dinghy with the outboard. It seemed to be coming straight for me. I think I felt something like a premonition of awfulness. Maybe it was the look on their faces. Stan Liddle, the youth club leader, and some bloke from the water-sport centre. They threw me a bright yellow rope, told me to hang on, said they'd tow me back to the landing jetty. Off we went, fast, my little canoe in the still water in between the wings of the dinghy's wash. The other canoes were bobbing and bouncing on the waves we'd made.

Apart from throwing me the rope and telling me to hang on, all Stan said was, "Your brother's come to collect you. I'm afraid it's serious." Which made me feel frantic, and absolutely clueless. And then Royston is standing there, shivering, blue lips, hunched shoulders, wet cheeks. Two words. "Dad's dead."

It was Kevin's dad who had driven Roy over. As soon as I'd convinced people there was no way I'd drink their sickly tea, we were gently shepherded into Mr McCleod's car – Roy and I both sharing the back seat. We drove home in an aching silence. No questions asked, no information offered. Nothing out loud.

I can remember crossing the river at Staines, the water crackling diamond bright, then past the mangy-looking Petters factory, crossing Runnymede, clipping the top end of Egham, up the steep bit of the A30 past Holloway College, huge and implausible on the left, turn right into St Jude's road, the final left into Bagshot Road. Each and every detail of that journey has been etched into my memory, and seems to stand as a solid reality, the polar opposite to the shocking truth which was just too grotesque to absorb.

So, at last to home. And there's my Ma, standing at the gate, arms folded, hands clamped tight under her armpits. She's standing there, waiting for me to get out of the car. I go straight to her and she hugs me, trembling. She allows herself a few lurching, shuddering sobs. Then she says, "We'll be alright. We're going to manage, somehow. I don't know how yet, but we're going to manage."

I'm a few weeks short of my fifteenth birthday, but I'm already a head taller than Ma. So she's saying this straight into my shoulder, as we stand there, hanging onto each other for dear life – incapable of absorbing the reality of a preposterous death. I feel as if I'm just too big for myself. I wanted to have my head nestled and cushioned within my Ma's embrace. But no, it's sticking out, exposed. The house and garden are there in vivid view whilst also, somehow, wrapped in a suffocating dream. I tell Ma and Royston, who's been hovering, that I'll come inside in a while. But first, I want to spend a few minutes in the garden. I feel an urgent need to pull some shabby dead-heads from the daffodils and primroses. Not really my job. Dad's job. But it gives me a reason to stay out and howl, without being directly watched or comforted.

I'm out there, perhaps for half-an-hour. I feel like I've wrung myself dry, for now, and that it's reasonably safe to risk going indoors. Ma and Royston are sitting in the kitchen, Ma at the table, Roy on top of the boiler, which he's just stoked and rattled. It's roaring, and in another couple of minutes, he'll have to get off to save his bum from roasting. The teapot sits on a mat in the middle of the table, wrapped up in the multi-coloured tail-end-of-the-wool-balls tea-cosy that Grandma had knitted. There's a half-full milk jug, the dark blue stoneware one, a bowl with the silver tongs and a few sugar-lumps, a remaining quarter of Ma's home-made Dundee cake, and three mugs. Theirs have dregs in the bottom, mine's clean and empty. Royston says, "Do you want a cupper, kiddo?" and I mumble "Not now." And Ma says, "Do you want to have something to eat? I don't know if it would be lunch or tea or whatever else" and I mumble another "Not now". And then just about manage to squeeze out a "Thanks."

I can't bear to be in the kitchen with them. I feel petrified that they will talk to me, tell me awful facts and terrible details about how Dad died. And I'm even more frightened that they'll ask me things, like how do I feel? And I really, really don't know. I mean, just what the fuck are you supposed to feel? There's been no rehearsal for this bastard. No stage directions. The truth is, apart from a weird sense of embarrassment, I don't think I feel anything. Not a single adjective comes to mind. I'm a blank. Can a person feel blank? I dunno! Close as I can get, it's blank plus the sort of numb that hurts. The numb you get when your leg goes to sleep, which you just know in advance has to be followed by painful pins and needles.

I tell them both that I'm going to lie down in my bedroom for a bit. They seem to approve this as a good idea. Once I'm in my room, protected by my closed door, lying full stretch on my bed, fingers interlocked behind my head, staring up at the ceiling, it comes to me.

It's a very clear, sharp picture of an open flesh wound. A diagonal gash across my belly. A long, deep cut. Skin, fat, blood, guts are all exposed. Open to the dangerous elements. And I see that there is no way to cover or close or protect this wound. Not at the moment. It will, unavoidably, all stay open from now until the funeral. So, for now, the more I can stay dead still, not moving a muscle or twitching an eye-lid, the safer I'll be. And I lie there, silent, almost motionless, imagining a priest saying some last rites, and a uniformed nurse, holding a giant sticking-plaster, preparing to patch me up, stick me back together again, to catch and keep the life that would otherwise simply ebb out of me.

Anyway, after what might have been ten minutes of lying there, scared and still, I simply fell asleep. Just as I was starting to drift off, I took one of the pillows from under my head, hugged it hard against my belly, rolled over on my left side, my face a foot from the wall. I might have slept for an hour – I'm not sure. I don't think I had any dreams whilst asleep. It was really the other way round. I felt OK the moment I woke up, but OK was very quickly replaced by a flash of anxious anticipation, then a sense of horror that the waking nightmare which had preceded this short respite in oblivion had been real and true then, and it's still real and true now. And no amount of tears and cursing will change it. And the other thing I remember, waking up after that nap, was feeling incredibly hungry. The smell of pork chops was wafting up to my bedroom from the kitchen. I wanted to run downstairs, burst into the kitchen, and announce that I could eat a herd of horses. And though I knew that I couldn't do that, I didn't have a clue about how to manage the ludicrous task of eating – which somehow felt as if it would belittle the serious business of grief. But we did eat. At least Royston and I did. Not Ma though. She pushed stuff around her plate a bit, then called the dog over, told her it was her lucky day, and scraped the lot into her bowl. She downed it in about twenty seconds, showing a complete lack of guilt, grief or remorse. So I whispered, quietly, to God and asked if I could swap myself and the mutt around. Let me be the dog, just for a while. But it felt like God wasn't listening, or couldn't be bothered with me.

Under my breath, I growled and barked for a bit.

The dog looked at me, askance. But she said nothing.

I can't remember clearly now. Maybe it was about a week, the time between getting that mental image of the open wound, and then having the actual funeral. However long it was, the bit which is clear in my mind is that the funeral was the necessary trigger that ushered in and then applied the almighty sticking plaster to patch me up and put me back together.

I'd not had broken ribs at that point in my life. But I have cracked and broken a few since. And there's something similar, a link joining busted bones and the feel of that plaster.

A few busted ribs will give you a significant level of background pain. You know they're there, grumbling away all the time – asleep or awake. And, in addition to the constant awareness, you become acutely self-protective. You walk, sit, stand and move about, in a totally different way. You wrap yourself in cotton wool. You can clearly anticipate some things as being a likely cause of extreme pain, and you avoid them at all costs. If you can. Some you can't. Like sneezing. When you realise that a sneeze is imminent and unavoidable, you grit your teeth, hold on, do it, then wince and whimper. That's how it felt. A background of pain, a lot of avoidance–where-possible, a layer of anaesthetic grief, wrapping and insulating and isolating me. Occasional stabs of hurt which felt unbearable, and everything slowed down. So for me, it was mostly a case of crawling along till we got to the funeral, which itself came to its inevitable conclusion, and then, after a fairly brief gathering at home, it was done.

As the last of the entourage left, I excused myself, went with absolutely conscious intent to my bedroom, lay full length on my bed, and pictured this vast sticking plaster being applied to me, covering the entirety of my split and protruding guts. And I felt better, and safer, immediately. And I felt absolutely sure, as soon as the plaster was stuck on, that I'd start to heal, there and then.

And that's pretty much what happened. Or at least, that's what I thought at the time.

Of course, I didn't realise, and nobody said back then, that there are things you have to do and check before applying the plaster. First of all, you have to make sure that the wound's clean, that you're not locking in stuff which will turn septic and putrefy.

And then you have to make sure that all the bits go back in their rightful places, not just shove them in anyhow, like stuffing a rucksack in a careless hurry. But I didn't know any of that, not then.

About a month after the funeral, we had two house guests. My great aunt from Wolverhampton (Ma's side) and my uncle, Dad's brother, who had recently arrived from India. Neither of them had been able to attend the funeral. Neither had met before. Ma introduced them to each other, in the sitting room. They shook hands, each of them looking drawn and desolate. My great aunt said, "I'm pleased to meet you, but sorry that it's in such awful circumstances." And I stood there, astonished. I think I actually said it out loud. Anyway, the voice was clear and shrill in my head. "What awful circumstances? What are you talking about?"

Followed by the inescapable realisation, "Oh, you mean Dad. But that was over a month ago. Why bring it up now?"

7

Fizz

I'm not clear about how Charley and Jack met. I think they probably bumped into each other in a Headingly pub. Casual chat over a couple of pints, that sort of thing. Anyway, they obviously got to know each other a bit. Enough for Jack to invite Charley to Little Flo's third birthday party. Jack probably wanted a bit of male company and moral support for himself. I doubt if he fancied being the only man there. Nine or ten local mums plus a dozen, two-, three- and four-year-olds. Jelly, ice-cream, pass the parcel. No surprise that Jack wanted a mate. Total shock that anyone would – well, that Charley did – accept the invitation. In fact, he swore blind that he wanted to come. Which he did. And he brought not just one, but two Cabbage Patch Dolls, each one nicely wrapped, and a card. Charley knew from Jack's description exactly where our house was, in St Claire Street, sandwiched between the Rugby Club and Ogden's Yard. Charley does loads of house calls, and he seems to know absolutely everywhere in Yorkshire.

Charley arrived at about quarter past three. Most of the kids and their mums were already here, and the party was in full flow. Sausage rolls and sandwiches, orange squash and fizzy pop. Candles, cake and ice-cream to follow. Jack introduced Charley, first to me, then Flo, then the other mums, then rest of the kids – most of whom Jack was unsure about, who belonged to who, who was called what. Charley gave me a short peck-on-the-cheek, and a lingering smile, and said he was delighted and had been looking forward to meeting me. He gave Little Flo her wrapped presents and card, which she held for a moment, then handed to me. Flo said nothing. I said nothing to her. Charley didn't seem flustered or embarrassed or ill-at-ease, unlike most people who meet Flo for the first time, and get themselves in a state, and seem to require directions from me or Jack about what to do or say. Not so with Charley. He picked her up in his arms, hugged her, told her she's the most beautiful three-years-old-today princess in Otley, that he was delighted to have been invited to her party, and that they would become best friends, straight away. Said he just knew it. And, amazingly, Flo went along, quite happily, from all appearances, with the whole thing. Extraordinary. Usually, if there's anyone who's a bit of an unknown to Little Flo, she'll keep her distance and go rigid if they try to get close. With Charley, she looked relaxed, almost warm. Not a word, of course. No hint of a response. Nothing you could describe as interaction. But something. Something about her gave the message "I feel OK with you, Charley."

We stuck to the basic party script. Musical statues, pass the parcel, pin the tail on the donkey. Really, it was for the other kids – who all joined in, like any normal toddlers would. Flo remained largely detached. But she watched, and kind-of joined in whenever Jack, or I, or Charley – once he'd seen how – held and guided her. The other kids made waves of excited noise. Flo stayed dead-pan, quite mute. But today, something almost like serene.

Charley was an absolute revelation He clearly loved the direct contact and involvement with the kids. He also had a great time swanning around with the mums. Dispensing tea and flattery in more or less equal portions. Spreading around a good vibe like a big picnic blanket on warm sand. What a hit. He helped us clear up and wash up after they'd all gone. Had some vaguely adult food – bangers, beans and mash – with me and Jack at 6.30 pm. Stayed in the kitchen while we bathed and read-to and bedded Flo. Stayed with me, still in the kitchen, at 7 o'clock, when Jack went off for his rugby training.

He said to me, more or less as soon as Jack's foot was out of the door, "So, Fizz, what's the story with Little Flo?" And I seemed to know as soon as he asked, that I'd be able to tell him the whole thing – as completely and as comfortably as I would have told it to my Mum.

I started at ten past seven, and three pots of tea, and three-and-a-bit hours later, I'd got us to the point of our present reality – pretty much settled in Otley – Jack studying, and loving all the Child Development and Psychology stuff – me being a full-time mum, and carer, and kind-of-counsellor, with Flo. I'd lightly skipped over my birthplace and background, explaining in broad terms how it's not only possible to be mixed-race and fully Jewish, to be born in Jamaica and to have a strong London accent, not only possible, but in my case, true.

But Charley's question was about Little Flo. So that's what I spent most time on. And my hunch was right. Better than right, Charley is one of the all-time greats to tell stuff to. Much better, in fact, than my Mum, who was always having to air her own views and her angles and her alternative options. But Charley just hoovers everything up, encouraging you to say more. Inviting you to either join the dots up in the picture you're painting, or accept that some realities are just unconnected random bits and bobs of life.

He's just repeated the question, 'So, what is the story with Flo?' and he's sitting back, cradling his mug of tea in both hands, his undivided attention focused on me, waiting without pushing. So I tell him. That Flo is only half the story. The other half is Nancy. Was Nancy. She was Flo's identical twin. They were delivered by C section, according to the plan, and everything was fine, almost too-good-to-be-true, at the hospital. We'd stayed there for the first week. Both of the babes were a picture of health, just under five pounds each, feeding well, no ventilators or incubators. Then home we all came. Happy as a bunch of Larry's. The twins were identical to look at. Even I could hardly tell them apart. But they weren't identical in character. Nancy was the dominant one. Born a few ounces heavier. Grew slightly quicker. First one to all the milestones, but only by a few days. Little Flo was forever catching Nancy up. But it was also as if Nancy knew to wait for her. And to help her along. Or share with her. And definitely, without a doubt, they had that twin telepathy thing going between them. We could tell from the day we brought them home. At times, they would do stuff in perfect unison – like those synchronised swimmers. We played games of taking them into separate rooms, and they just carried on in separated synch even when they couldn't hear or see each other. They certainly appeared to be happy and content when they were together. And they definitely got stressed and anxious any time we prised them apart by more than a few yards.

And as I'm telling Charley about this cute and cosy pair of kids, I can feel the dark shadow approach. So, I jump straight out of nostalgia and dive head-first – heaven to hell in one easy step.

I tell him. Just blurt it out. Nancy died in her sleep. No warning, no illness, no preparation for that bombshell. They shared a room, but each had her own cot. It was Jack who found Nancy, lying there half-covered with her blanket, stone cold. Little Flo was standing up at her bars, staring intently at Nancy, but dead quiet. In fact, it was the quiet which had got to Jack. It was nearly eight o'clock, and usually, the pair of them would've been chattering for at least an hour. Jack said he was terrified before he picked her up. Said she looked too still and the wrong colour. She was a bit stiff, and stone cold. He held her to his face. Then he ran into our room with her, shouting, "There's something badly wrong with Nancy. She's cold all over." And he gave her to me, believing I'd know what to do, how to make her better.

And I knew it, immediately, that it was useless, but I told him anyway, "Go downstairs, and call an ambulance." So he went off, then came back after a couple of minutes to tell me, "They're on their way", and he asked, "What do you think is wrong with her?", and I said, "Jack, I think she's dead," and he just kept saying "No, she can't be, she can't possibly be." Then I told him, "Go and get Flo, and get her dressed and take her out for a walk." Which is what he did. And she never uttered a sound, all that morning, all that day. And she's never really been the same, or said anything since.

8

Fizz

Telling Charley the answer to his question of "What's the story with Little Flo?" has brought it all back, and now the whole thing is just stuck, as if it's a ball of barbed wire, stuck in my throat, and it won't go down and I can't sick it up or spit it out...

What a bloody nightmare. The second they got back from the park and Jack walked in with Flo, and saw the police, he looked as if he was about to blow up. They'd been gone probably for a couple of hours, sitting by the river apparently, watching the ducks.

The ambulance had come about ten minutes after Jack had phoned for them. He'd managed to get Flo out with maybe a couple of minutes to spare. I heard the ambulance drive up – no screaming sirens, thank God. I opened the front door just as they were about to ring the bell. Two of them. One a big bloke with red hair and freckles all over his face and hands. The other, an older woman, forty something, small and neat, Scottish accent. She spoke first. "Is this the baby?"

I was holding Nancy, wrapped up in her pink blanket. I said, "Yes. Come in." We all walked into the sitting room. She said, "My name's Marie. This is Andrew. Let's have a look at the wee bairn then." I didn't want to let go of Nancy, but Marie just gently took her from me, laid her on the sofa, unwrapped her, felt her neck, forehead, face. Put the stethoscope on her lifeless chest. Told me what I already knew, but couldn't believe.

Marie looked up from Nancy to me.

"I'm afraid she's gone. She's probably been dead for a couple of hours, maybe more. There's nothing we can do to save her now. So sorry."

I stared at Marie and wished, with all my might that my heart, instead of giving me this useless, searing pain, would just stop beating altogether, and I could join Nancy in her icy dark emptiness. After what felt like ages, I started to breathe again. And then I did some yelling and screaming. Andrew took hold of me. He smelt a bit of stale sweat, which somehow felt like a kind of comfort. He let me go after a while. I couldn't look him in the eye. Just stared at his shirt, noticing I'd left a wet patch of tears and a trace of snot. Marie said, "Was it your husband who phoned for the ambulance?" I said yes it was, and that he'd taken Little Flo, Nancy's twin sister, out, to save her from seeing all this.

Andrew asked if there was anyone who could be with me now, and I said not to worry, because Jack and Flo would be back soon. Then Marie told me that they would be contacting the police and I asked what for and she said, "It's what we have to do."

So, off they went, taking my dead baby with them, leaving me alone in the house. Well, alone apart from Marley, who whined a little bit, looked at me, then slinked off to her basket and curled up in silence, barely able to look at me.

I swore, briefly but viciously, at my Mum, for not being there. But, other than that little outburst, the rest's a blank. How long I was there, what I did, or what, if anything, was going on in my head, I have no idea.

I didn't hear the police car coming. Wasn't expecting that. The doorbell rang. I thought it must have been Jack who'd forgotten his keys. I opened the door and was startled to see the two of them. Uniformed officers, standing there, asking to come in. Less than a minute after I'd shown them into the front room, Jack and Flo were there too.

I knew a little bit about Jack's previous with the police, but not the whole story, not then.

He looked haunted when he walked into the room, but then the sight of the two uniforms, both men, seemed to transform his grief into rage. He looked ready to erupt. I felt sick and scared. Thank God, the uniforms kept their mouths shut for that moment, which gave me the chance to get into a hug with Jack, and tell him I needed him to hold me close, which he just about managed, though he felt stiff and awkward, as if we were complete strangers.

When Jack and I have a standing-up hug, my head comes to somewhere around the top of his belly. So, unless I turn my head to the side, I don't get to see much. I did turn my head, and I caught a glimpse of Little Flo, sitting strapped in to her buggy, eyes like saucers, motionless, dead pan. She didn't look like herself at all. She looked like her soul had been ripped out of her heart, leaving a dry husk. I was just lost, and, literally, didn't know which way to turn. Don't think I'd ever felt so helpless. I certainly didn't want to leave Jack alone with the police. But I couldn't bear to leave Flo strapped in and unheld. And I knew that I didn't want her in the room with the police while they were asking their questions.

Holy shit.

Then this picture came into my head. I was that rabbit stuck in the headlights. But there are two sets of them. From two enormous trucks, both charging towards me from opposite directions. It looks nasty.

Without another thought, I make a grab for Flo, all fingers and fumbling thumbs, unbuckle her, lift her up, and say I have to take her upstairs. I tell Jack that he'll have to deal with the police. I say they should all have tea, and bolt out of the room.

9

I can't understand anything that's happening. What's going on? Why am I doing this?

Why am I getting Little Flo dressed and rushed out of the house, as if she and I are a pair of criminals, fleeing the scene of some terrible crime?

Why are we rushing out of the house? Well, because Fizz told me to, with a voice and a tone that sounded as if she knew what to do and why. I didn't have a clue. In fact, I felt as if I'd been spiked with some ghastly acid trip which was throwing me head-first into a horror movie. I thought I was going to pass out.

I was sweating buckets, had a pounding heart and a throbbing head. I felt like I was going to puke and piss and crap myself all at the same time in a stinking evacuation of belly and bladder and bowels.

Somehow, I got Flo into her clothes, into her buggy and out of the front door. As soon as we were outside, the cool air toned down the sickly feeling, replacing it with a dry mouth and teeth chattering shivers. But, if anything, the sense of unreality just kept growing.

We walked through the town, and sat down on a bench in Titty Bottle Park, looking at the swans and ducks bobbing about on the river. And that stupid bloody name, Titty Bottle Park, just kept echoing and rattling round in my mind. Usually, it raised a bit of a smile, bringing to mind pictures of the Edwardian families who had christened it when the park first opened. But now, it was a ghoulish refrain, mocking the prospect of happy families enjoying their care-free outing. Titty Bottle was one half of my mental chorus line. The other half was Fizz saying, "I think she's dead." How could Fizz think she's dead. There was nothing wrong with her. There wasn't anything which could possibly have harmed her in the cot. She went to bed warm and pink and full of chattering baby banter, just like Flo. She couldn't possibly have gone from perfectly healthy to dead without being ill in-between. Not possible. But, when I picked her up, I knew, immediately, that the life had gone from her. Before I'd even felt her cold little body. Before I'd realised she wasn't breathing. Her spirit had just disappeared.

It was obvious.

And it was ridiculous.

Couldn't be true.

Couldn't be escaped.

We just sat there, in the park, me and Flo. I kept looking at her, every few seconds, checking. And she sat there, haunted, wide-eyed, not looking at, or seeing anything.

I didn't say a word to her, because I was terrified that I might suddenly jolt her out of her trance, and give her a shock which would break her little heart.

I couldn't bear to be away from Fizz for any longer. But I didn't dare to go home, to face the grisly reality which awaited us. So we stayed there, gripped in this sick torture. That is, until we saw Chris, my new mate from the rugby club. He'd spotted us from fifty yards away, gave us a cheerful wave, and was walking straight towards us.

I twirled the buggy around, and we trundled off home, fast, head down, full to the brim with misery.

I don't know what I'd been expecting on our return. Maybe a miracle. Finding Nancy warm and well, cradled in her mum's arms, both of them smiling. Discovering it had all been some dreadful mistake. Or a sick prank. Or else, finding a team of doctors and nurses, tubes and equipment everywhere, all joined in a heroic effort to bring her back, a magical snatch from the jaws of cruel death.

Or Fizz, all alone, desolate, broken.

I'd had a fair bunch of alternative scenes-in-the-head, and I'd been seriously begging God, trying to bargain, promising him all sorts, offering any deal if he'd just give Nancy her life back, and re-unite Little Flo with her essential other half.

But, the reality, when we did get home, was two uniformed policemen, large as life, standing there in my front room. Just what the fuck was that about? I was ready and willing to explode with God-knows-what, when Fizz grabbed hold of me, and told me she needed a hug, which I gave her. Well, sort of. But I was looking, hard-eyed, at the pair of them, and they were looking back at me, stony-faced, no sign of sympathy, not that I saw. Then I felt something shift inside Fizz. She drew away from me, and she said she had to take Flo upstairs, and asked me to make a pot of tea for everyone. What flashed into my head was that other memory, the sickly taste of the over-sweetened tea they'd tried to force on me when Roy told me about Dad.

Anyway, Fizz and Flo left the room, without a backward glance from either of them. I was full to bursting, with anguish and seething anger. I looked directly at the two Bills, and said, "What are you doing here? What do you want?" And the bigger one said, "Why don't we sit down?", and I said, "Why don't the pair of you just FUCK OFF out of my house and leave us in peace?" And then the smaller one chipped in, "Because there are some questions we have to ask, and you need to answer, before we're going anywhere." They didn't sound friendly, and didn't look nice. Tea, at that point, was definitely off the menu. An outburst of violent rage seemed a much more likely prospect.

And just at that precise moment, the doorbell rang, which probably saved the carpet from getting blood spattered, and me from being arrested for another offence of Old Bill battery.

Fizz shouted from upstairs, "Jack, can you get the door, I'm busy with Flo," and I thought she sounded a bit weird – even in the middle of all the madness that was filling the house. A bit weird. But I just yelled back "Yep," and felt relieved that I had to leave the room for a minute.

I opened the door to someone who immediately introduced herself as Miss Florence Sinclair, and said that she was a social worker, and had been told about Nancy's death. She said that she was sorry for our loss, that she guessed that we all must be in a terrible state of shock and she asked if she could come in. She said all this in the soft and soothing tones of a well-educated Jamaican. And, apart from Fizz, she was the only black person I'd ever seen in Otley.

It was immediately obvious to me that she had arrived, on cue, as my personal guardian angel.

I told her my name, said that Fizz and Flo were upstairs, and that there were two policemen in the front room. To which she said, "Yes, Mr Warren, I know."

Then I offered her my shaky hand, which she took and held in both of hers, and she said "A'right'" twice, classic Jamaican pronunciation, no L.

Once we got into the front room, Florence asked if she might take the weight off her aching feet. I said, "Of course, please." So first she, and then we all sat down, calm and polite.

All was quiet for a brief moment, and it felt as if a hint of peace had come into the room. Florence exuded this amazing aura of serenity, sending out a calmness which we all just soaked up as if it was a rain shower on a parched lawn. She took a long, deep breath, then she told it straight.

She said that the paramedics had noticed one fresh scratch, and three older-looking bruises on Nancy's face and neck. And then some more around her chest when they were searching for her heartbeat. They had reported these as possible non-accidental injuries, and therefore a potential Child Protection issue. A post-mortem would be required in order to try to ascertain the cause of death. She said that the fact that I had taken Little Flo out of the house meant that she, on behalf of the Social Services Department, had an urgent duty to ensure that Flo herself was unharmed, safe, and faced no likely danger.

Florence managed to say all of this without any hint of accusation. Straight away, I told her that I understood, and promised my full co-operation with the whole process of investigation. The two Bills sat there, silent, but slightly softened.

We all paused, to take a breath and gather our thoughts.

My own thought didn't arrive immediately or fully formed. It emerged with growing substance, like a big rock on a misty heath, which gradually reveals itself with every approaching step.

Here's how it took form. Firstly, the Old Bill are notified of an unexplained infant's death – no preceding illness or obvious cause. Then the paramedics add in some recent, plus some older-looking, bangs and bruises. They, the Bills, then check out the family, only to find that the Daddy has got form, namely a previous history of mental health problems, a period inside a secure psychiatric unit, and a conviction for a violent assault on a police officer, and then Daddy does a runner with the other toddler to avoid seeing the ambulance folk. Only comes back when he thinks the coast has cleared. He definitely looks and sounds aggressive when he meets the uniformed officers, and invites them both to fuck off out of his house.

If I didn't know me better I'd have been suspicious. I took some more deep breaths, and then I offered to make tea for us all.

10

Fizz

As soon as I'd got Flo in my arms, and closed the sitting room
door behind us, I knew that I just had to concentrate on her,
and leave Jack and the police to it. It felt like I was holding some
stranger's kid, someone who didn't know or trust me. Somehow,
Flo felt as limp and lifeless as a rag doll. And, at the same time,
as fragile as a light-bulb. I carried her upstairs, and stood on the
landing, dithering over which bedroom to go into, ours or hers. I
moved towards hers and reached for the door handle. As soon as
I touched it, I felt this massive electric shock. But then I realised,
it hadn't come from the door handle. It was Flo, pumping out

fear and alarm from every pore of her clammy skin.

So we went into our room and sat on the bed, both of trembling, me out of breath.

I can't explain or understand what happened next. And I've never said a word about it to anyone. It's as if I feel ashamed about it. But in my memory, the whole scene is clear, and slowed down. Like we were both in a trance. I shifted Flo in my left arm, undid the top three buttons of my blouse, uncupped my left breast from the bra and offered it to her. She latched on, and began to suck, gently and rhythmically. I don't know if any milk came through, but it felt like something beyond just feeding, as if I was offering her the chance to restore a bit of life back into her poor empty shell. And for a few precious, priceless minutes, we seemed to both be at peace, safe from the nightmare which had gate crashed our lives.

But there was no lasting salvation. No real escape. Our brief moment of sanctuary was ripped apart by the ring of the doorbell, which made me jump, almost out of my skin, and made Flo jump too. She clenched her teeth, hard, biting into my nipple. There was a stabbing pain, which I only just managed to feel, as if it was happening to someone else who I barely knew.

I shouted down to Jack, telling him to get the door.

Our tranquil spell had been smashed to bits. Flo returned to her fragile light-bulb feel. And I felt exposed, and something like ashamed. I was blushing from head to toe, beads of sweat itching round my forehead and upper lip, rank, clammy armpits, wet and shameful between my legs. Dry mouth. Furry tongue. Revolting.

As for Flo, not a peep. Hatches battened down. Total retreat.

I suppose I was vaguely aware of Jack talking to someone at the front door but couldn't make out what was being said. But then a single word drifted up the stairs and into our room. Followed by a short pause. Then a repetition, slightly longer and louder, "A'right," Pure Jamaican, just like my Mum. It was the last word she ever said. I thought I must have imagined it.

We stayed put, me and Flo. She was rigidly stiff and totally still. I was uncomfortable, awkward, with an aching back. Locked in silence, head swirling with bitter words and nasty pictures.

Later, a soft knock on the bedroom door, which gently opened before I'd even managed a reply. This gorgeous face appeared, and said, "Hello, Mrs Warren, my name is Florence Sinclair, I'm a social worker. Your husband said it would be alright for me to come upstairs to see you and Flo. Please may I come in?" I nodded, and I think, well I hope, that I smiled. I hope I gave her some sign of how good it felt to see her. Anyway, in she came. She said hello directly to Flo, and told her that she believed they shared the same name.

The bedroom was a bit messy, but really, not too bad. I popped Flo under the eiderdown, tucking it up to her chin, arms out, head propped by two pillows. It was like arranging one of those bendy toys, the ones that keep whatever shape you put them in.

I said "Excuse me" to Florence whilst I removed the small pile of clean clothes from the one comfy chair in the room, and placed them in the corner. Then I invited her to sit down, whilst I sat at the foot of the bed, opposite her, Nancy's pink blanket still draped round my shoulders.

Florence said, "I understand your family comes from Jamaica?" and I nodded, and said "Yes, they did, and plenty of them still live there." She asked which parish and I told her Mandeville, and she said it was her original home too, and that no doubt we have some relatives in common, but that was stuff for another time. Then she sat back, gave a long sigh, folded her hands in her lap, and began.

"OK, Mrs Warren. First, I need you to tell me about what happened this morning up to the time your husband phoned for the ambulance. Then what happened between that call and when the police arrived. And after that, we'll take a look at Flo together. Mr Warren's downstairs with the policemen. They're having tea, and they're all just fine now. You can take your time."

So, I told her the whole sorry story, although it felt like my voice wasn't my own, and that it was about a different family altogether. And she said, "Mmm" and "OK" and "a'right", and every now and then she exactly repeated my words back to me, checking the facts and the sequence. All the time, as I was talking, she kept looking past me at Flo, who hardly moved a muscle. Florence asked me if Flo was usually this quiet, and I told her no, the exact opposite actually, and Florence said she thought that Flo was in a state of deep shock. But that the reaction was understandable and normal. She said it probably wouldn't last long, and not to worry.

She never said it might last for years.

12

Before we were able to organise the funeral, we had the ordeal of the post-mortem business to get through. Sure enough, that was gruelling, but it culminated with a verdict of a cot death, so no blame, nobody culpable, just an ordinary little tragedy. After the whole palaver with the Coroner's Court, Fizz and I were united in the belief that Nancy's funeral was the centrepiece of the most awful day of our lives. It was some competition, but in the end, no contest.

Not many people attended. We'd only been living in Otley for about six months, so had just a few new friends. I'd joined

11

You know that feeling, when you meet someone new, and you're quite sure you've never seen them before in your life, but there's something about them which is deeply familiar, and has that sense of being safe and known. Well, that's what I had with Florence, from the moment I clapped eyes on her. I felt this big, powerful hint in that first instant of encounter, which turned into a rock-solid confirmation when she took hold of my hand in both of hers. I knew that she brought to mind someone who had been a crucial part of my life. Just couldn't think who it was.

The answer was almost there, right on the tip of my brain, but the connection was a tantalising inch beyond my grasp.

It came to me, later that night. Marley and I were sitting together on the sofa. Even she seemed to have been poisoned by the misery that was hanging over the entire house like a stinking shroud. No mad antics from the poor pooch. She asked, almost apologetically, to go out for a walk at about nine o'clock. Had a perfunctory pee, then turned back for home.

Earlier on, we'd moved little Flo's cot into our bedroom, putting it right next to the Fizz side of the bed. We gave her a bath at seven, tucked her in at ten past. Fizz said that she was exhausted, and just wanted to lie down and rest, but she couldn't sleep. Every time I went into check, she was lying there fully alert, watching Flo, their heads no more than a foot apart.

As for me, I was so agitated and twitchy that I couldn't even think of lying in bed, so I sat downstairs, and smoked one pointless joint after another.

Time for Mozart. The Clarinet Quintet. The first move-ment soothed, like cool cream on sunburned skin. Then the andante really did it, burst open the floodgates, and out gushed the pent-up torrent of tears. As soon as the third movement started, I turned it off. I was no way ready for hope or redemption yet. I just lay there, mostly spent, staring up at the ceiling. It was covered in those white polystyrene tiles, one of which had a double dent in it – the imprint of two flamboyantly popped champagne corks which we'd fired off the day the twins were born. My Ma had turned each indentation into the centre of a flower, surrounded with big bright red petals, drawn in felt tip.

Underneath, the inscription, "Nancy and Flo. Born at noon, 08/08/73. A perfect pair."

Not anymore. A pair no longer. Paradise lost.

I had to close my eyes. The grief was more than enough to blind me. I just lay there a while longer, doing weeping and wailing, plus occasional full body-shudders, and those inhales that come with the stutters.

And then, quite suddenly, I got the connection. I saw the uniforms of the Old Bills who'd been here earlier. Blue uniforms.

Blue uniforms and white coats. My stint in the Adolescent Unit. The silent battles and the pent-up rage against the White Coats, resolved, dissolved by Dr M, who wore no uniform, but held my hand, and walked me away from the edge of the abyss.

So, as my Ma would say, "Who'd've thunk it?" Dr M an Miss Florence Sinclair. A pair of perfect opposites. Black an white, large and lean, now and then. And yet they were unit absolutely as one, in their extraordinary capacity to create, an hold open a space for a light to appear in the darkest pit of desp the rugby club the month before, but was still very much the odd outsider there. And anyway, it was not really the scene for male macho, a tiny tot's funeral, although, to his credit, Chris did come, and wept like a six–and–a-half foot baby.

Fizz had lost her mum three years earlier, never had much to do with her dad since she was a toddler, and never took to her stepdad.

Roy and his family were living in America, so they were no-shows. My Ma was there, plus my stepdad. Fizz got in touch with some distant cousin who lives in Bradford, and she turned up. So, as far as family goes, that was it. Us two plus three. Barely a dozen for the whole wake. Pitiful. Maybe apt too.

The service was held in Bridge Church. Started at 2 pm. All done in a bit over half-an-hour. It was one of those bright and breezy autumn days. Warm whilst the sun was out, chilly every time the white cotton clouds interrupted the rays. The stained-glass windows gave an impressive show of dazzling light and sombre shade.

The vicar was nice, and not much older than us. He came round a couple of days before the service. Had tea. Asked us about our preference for hymns. We told him we preferred not. Didn't explain why. So, he asked if there was any other music we'd like.

Fizz said that she likes Mozart, and that I'm nuts about him. We thought about a bit of the Requiem, but then thought not. Settled for the slow movement in the Clarinet Quintet. When I told Ma the next day, she said that it was a perfect choice. Said she believed that poor broken-hearted Wolfy had written it whilst he was grieving over the death of his baby daughter. Ma knows her stuff about music, about where it comes from, and how it can captivate the soul, and how it can cradle broken hearts.

So, one exquisite piece from the genius. But we were stuck, for a while, to choose what else.

The vicar – call me Gary – said that anything we'd got, or could get onto tape, he could play. Quite a few blues numbers came to mind, with snatches of lyrics crying about "Baby's gone now," but they all felt wrong. And then Fizz said, "What about something from the Incredible String Band? You're always singing their stuff." Which is true.

No sooner said, than up it popped, ping, into my mind, like the price tag on a cash till. And that was it, the song that brought the curtain down. October Song.

At 2.35 on October 15th, 1974, this is how we said goodbye to Nancy, and sent her on her way:

> I'll sing you this October song
> Though there is no one before it
> The words and notes are none of my own
> For my joys and sorrows bore it.
> The autumn leaves that jewel the ground
> They know the art of dying
> Birds cry out their sad farewells
> And with them I'd be flying.

Night-night Nancy. Sweet dreams.

13

My first few weeks at Beecliffe felt like a potent mixture of weird and wearisome, but were generally lacking in wonderful. Immediately after the move Fizz was absolutely clear that my presence was required at home whilst we got sorted with the plumbing-in of the washing machine, the wiring-up of the cooker and the unpacking of a seemingly endless mountain range of cardboard boxes. Flo was fretful, so I ended up with her whilst Fizz did the practical business of setting up home. A kind of interim order emerged after three or four days.

We were having tea on Wednesday afternoon, when

Marley heard the rattle of the letterbox and let off a volley of ear-shattering barking. I went to investigate, and found an envelope with my name on it, lying on the mat. Its contents comprised a hand-written note plus another double-folded sheet. "Dear Jack, hope you've settled in. Here's your rota. See you at eight tomorrow morning. It was signed Barry Stanger, Team Leader of Spearman House, one of the three non-secure Assessment Units.

Sweet Jesus. Talk about in at the deep end.

I arrived at Spearman at eight on the dot, and encountered a line of thirteen kids in the corridor. Barry was there. He gave me a rather curt, "Good morning, Mr Warren. This lot are ready, but Casey is being difficult, come and give me a hand." So, I accompanied Barry into the six-bedded dorm, where we encountered the cloying stench of urine, and Casey, half-concealed under a bed, hanging on to one of its metal legs with both hands. Barry addressed his protruding lower half. "Right, Casey, everyone else is lined up. You are keeping us waiting. I've already asked you to move. Now, Mr Warren and I are going to remove you."

A voice rolled out from beneath the bed. "You can fucking try if you like."

Barry sighed with menace. "Mr Warren, which end of Casey would you prefer to take?" Perhaps unwisely, I chose the apparently more available leg end, which immediately began to kick out with obviously well-practised skill and violence. After a brief, messy and for me, painful tussle, I'd got a decent grip, locking his knees and ankles together under my left arm, closing the vice with my right. I'd been so immersed in my end of the manoeuvre that I hadn't managed to see the full precision of Barry's technique. But in outline, it involved the whole bed going up in the air, briefly, then crashing down, forcefully, and after a rather stomach-churning thud, and a teeth-clenched comment of "You fucking bastard", the remaining half of Casey emerged, blinking, into daylight, with one arm pinned to his side, and the other one quite a long way up his back.

We all remained there, panting, for perhaps half a minute. Then Barry said, "OK Casey, what's it to be? Breakfast, or shall we go straight to sick bay where you can have an injection?" Casey said "Breakfast, please sir." And, after the briefest pause, added, "I'm alright. I'll walk, sir."

He joined the queue, and off we all went. Single file, a well-behaved and most obedient crocodile.

After breakfast, a rather disheartening affair – weak tea, lumpy porridge, and toast like cardboard, Barry asked me if I knew where sick bay was. I told him I did, so he asked me if I could accompany Casey there for him to get his medication, which he subsequently took, meek as a lamb. Twenty-five mils of bright orange Largactyl syrup. Having swallowed it, he gave me a wink and said, "Didn't fancy that needle in my arse this morning. Fucking hurts." And I told him that I could imagine.

Didn't say I remember it well.

We all arrived in the gym at nine o'clock for assembly. Crocodiles converged from various points of the campus for the start of the school day. Ken Kaminsky was there as the master of ceremonies. No hymns or prayers. Just the abrupt allocation of kids into classes, bits of educational assessment for some, post-assessment teaching for others. I watched, vaguely amused, initially thinking myself to be an innocent bystander. Then Ken said, "Mr Warren. Your first day in school. Welcome. You've got the pre-assessment maths group till break, then the English group till lunch. End of the corridor. Last door on the left."

That was it, and off we went.

They could smell it on me. A potent cocktail. A mixture of fear, ignorance and exasperation. They could all see that I didn't have a clue, where anything was, who anyone was, what on earth I was supposed to do with them. They looked at me, looked at each other, and a ripple of not-so-nice laughter went round the room. All I could think was, "Oh shit."

Casey broke the ensuing pointed silence, by asking me if I had a key for the stationery cupboard. I told him I'd been given a basic set, but didn't have a clue which was which. He asked me if he could try, so I threw him the bunch and said, "Help yourself." He immediately found the right one, opened the door and chucked the keys back to me. He then said to the class, "Right lads, someone wake me up at break time OK? And don't take the piss out of Sir." And with that, he removed a few exercise books from the top shelf, put them on the floor as his pillow, and laid himself down, with his feet poking out of the door.

One of the other lads said, "He always sleeps in the cupboard for the first couple of lessons. It's the drugs." Others nodded. I said, "Sounds fair enough. How about the rest of us working out ten different ways of spending twenty pounds, and once we've done that, we'll have a quiz." No-one said no way, so that's what we did.

12

Before we were able to organise the funeral, we had the ordeal of the post-mortem business to get through. Sure enough, that was gruelling, but it culminated with a verdict of a cot death, so no blame, nobody culpable, just an ordinary little tragedy. After the whole palaver with the Coroner's Court, Fizz and I were united in the belief that Nancy's funeral was the centrepiece of the most awful day of our lives. It was some competition, but in the end, no contest.

Not many people attended. We'd only been living in Otley for about six months, so had just a few new friends. I'd joined

Underneath, the inscription, "Nancy and Flo. Born at noon, 08/08/73. A perfect pair."

Not anymore. A pair no longer. Paradise lost.

I had to close my eyes. The grief was more than enough to blind me. I just lay there a while longer, doing weeping and wailing, plus occasional full body-shudders, and those inhales that come with the stutters.

And then, quite suddenly, I got the connection. I saw the uniforms of the Old Bills who'd been here earlier. Blue uniforms.

Blue uniforms and white coats. My stint in the Adolescent Unit. The silent battles and the pent-up rage against the White Coats, resolved, dissolved by Dr M, who wore no uniform, but held my hand, and walked me away from the edge of the abyss.

So, as my Ma would say, "Who'd've thunk it?" Dr M and Miss Florence Sinclair. A pair of perfect opposites. Black and white, large and lean, now and then. And yet they were united, absolutely as one, in their extraordinary capacity to create, and to hold open a space for a light to appear in the darkest pit of despair.

The answer was almost there, right on the tip of my brain, but the connection was a tantalising inch beyond my grasp.

It came to me, later that night. Marley and I were sitting together on the sofa. Even she seemed to have been poisoned by the misery that was hanging over the entire house like a stinking shroud. No mad antics from the poor pooch. She asked, almost apologetically, to go out for a walk at about nine o'clock. Had a perfunctory pee, then turned back for home.

Earlier on, we'd moved little Flo's cot into our bedroom, putting it right next to the Fizz side of the bed. We gave her a bath at seven, tucked her in at ten past. Fizz said that she was exhausted, and just wanted to lie down and rest, but she couldn't sleep. Every time I went into check, she was lying there fully alert, watching Flo, their heads no more than a foot apart.

As for me, I was so agitated and twitchy that I couldn't even think of lying in bed, so I sat downstairs, and smoked one pointless joint after another.

Time for Mozart. The Clarinet Quintet. The first movement soothed, like cool cream on sunburned skin. Then the andante really did it, burst open the floodgates, and out gushed the pent-up torrent of tears. As soon as the third movement started, I turned it off. I was no way ready for hope or redemption yet. I just lay there, mostly spent, staring up at the ceiling. It was covered in those white polystyrene tiles, one of which had a double dent in it – the imprint of two flamboyantly popped champagne corks which we'd fired off the day the twins were born. My Ma had turned each indentation into the centre of a flower, surrounded with big bright red petals, drawn in felt tip.

11

You know that feeling, when you meet someone new, and you're quite sure you've never seen them before in your life, but there's something about them which is deeply familiar, and has that sense of being safe and known. Well, that's what I had with Florence, from the moment I clapped eyes on her. I felt this big, powerful hint in that first instant of encounter, which turned into a rock-solid confirmation when she took hold of my hand in both of hers. I knew that she brought to mind someone who had been a crucial part of my life. Just couldn't think who it was.

14

My working life gradually came into focus as a bunch of almost parallel universes which, somehow occasionally touched, yet regularly seemed to contradict each other. There were occasional bits of sublime, and, I thought, lots of ridiculous.

There was definitely an almighty clash of cultures going on. Lots of what went on at Beecliffe was genuine, dyed-in-the-wool, old-school. A virtually all-male staff team, most of whom had been there for donkey's years. They shared an almost unanimous conviction that they'd seen and done it all before, and that they didn't need, or want to learn anything new or different about how to manage a bunch of kids whose essential characteristics were of being difficult, dangerous, and, given half a chance, unbelievably disruptive. The provision of "firm but fair boundaries", clear rules, and strict discipline – these were the hallmarks, and the official euphemisms, of the old-school approach. The realities were often simply brutal. Night-time disruption would be met with the threat, and regular enactment, of summary violence. Kids would be marched, barefoot along frozen paths, to the gym, and required to get down on hands and knees to scrub the floor with toothbrushes. Every morning, the "enuretics", the miserable and maligned bed-wetters, would be required to walk across the all-weather pitch, carrying their soggy sheets to the laundry, in acts of public humiliation. At the first sign of any group challenge to staff authority, ring-leaders would be identified and "taken down a peg or two." In many ways, it was like the culture of the public school, reliant on systemic bullying and a range of commonplace cruelties. But, these kids were certainly not seen as the future governors of empire and captains of industry. Rather, they were decried as the scrapings from the bottom of the barrel, destined for lives of waste, crime and sporadic imprisonment.

There was an awful lot of not nice.

And yet.

And yet there was an altogether more humane, and gentle and endearing side. A nurturing maternal vein, contrasting so starkly with the male testosterone-driven chauvinist piggery of power abused.

Bobby Zimmerman had told us, well over a decade earlier, that the times they were a-changin'. But for sure, it was many a mile of painfully slow crawling up the A1 before that message got to Beecliffe, and even once it had arrived, there were an awful lot of dyed-in-the-wools, whose attitudes affirmed that any changes would have to be accomplished over their dead bodies.

Dr Aveyleigh was the irrepressible force for change, pitting himself against the immovable objects of obstinate and ingrained conservatism. The fact that he was an astute political operator who had succeeded in getting millions in government money to build his new secure unit and a whole cohort of newly appointed staff, meant that the wind of change he brought was rattling the windows and shaking the foundations of the old-school establishment. His sails billowed out with momentum, and his sleek prow cut through the waves, albeit like a bulldozer. It was a time of great churning.

And what a stunning chasm – the gap between the realities as discussed and debated around the conference-room table and the feel of daily life in the classrooms, the unit dorms and kids' common rooms. I'm not sure whether it should be a source of pride or shame, but the reality for me was that I seemed to be able to fit with comfort and ease into both of these contradicting realities.

In particular, I felt at ease when it was the show-time of Assessment Review meetings. I enjoyed the art and craft of report-writing, and developed a talent for portraying the subjects of these Assessments in a way that somehow seemed to capture bits of their essence, like the snapshot which defines a face and also reveals its heart. I was definitely captivated by the idea that someone's personality, and character, and indeed their current and latent potential – all could be systematically profiled. And once that profile was revealed, the judicious application of remedies for problems, and the enhancement of talents could, quite dramatically, change lives. Save lives.

All of which, at least on a good day, felt like a great source for optimism. The notion that warped minds and wayward hearts could all be mended. These were bright rays of theoretical sunshine. But on the not-so-good days, such fond hopes were dashed on the unrelenting rocks of classroom lessons or late shifts on the units, in which real-life flesh-and-all-too-bloody kids made mayhem, and were often treated with casual disdain and thoughtless cruelties.

Plus, for me personally, there was a great big chunk of "what's more." Namely, the realisation that the process and the protocols of assessment were not necessarily restricted to those young people placed within the Assessment Centre. They provided a microscope and dissection kit which could be applied, most interestingly, to colleagues at work, to the dynamics of staff teams, to friends, foes and families. How exciting and fascinating.

And (with the clarity of belated but eventual hindsight, I am simply amazed at the length of time it took me to realise this) with a little less smoke and a bit more mirror, I could start to use those tools of investigation to seriously look at myself.

15

It must have been about eleven months after I'd started at Beecliffe when I got my first "really big deal" Assessment Review meeting. Presumably Dr Aveyleigh thought that my gestation period was done, and I was ready to stand – well, sit, really – and deliver. I'd already popped out a couple of dozen lesser creations, the also-rans of the Beecliffe report genre. I'd done maybe half a crate's worth of returned empties. Namely, those kids who were back for re-assessment, plus a whole bunch where the placement recommendations were mere overstatements of the blindingly bleeding obvious – those kids who everyone knew, from the moment they'd set foot in the centre, were destined for placements at our local bog-standard training schools, or a spell in a detention centre. Dr Aveyleigh tended not to waste his precious time on such mundane fare, and left them to be rubber-stamped on their ways by Ken Kaminsky or the mere mortal deputies.

So, for me, this was the big one, the first Assessment Report which I was to present to His Eminence. It was unusual on a couple of counts. Firstly, he, the subject of the report, was a boy from a well-off Jewish family, who had caused a bit of actual bodily harm to his daddy. He'd sliced into a piece of his Pop with a bread knife, leaving a six-inch gash from clavicle to sternum, though only achieving an inch or so of superficiality. No rib penetration to the heart of that matter. Apart from the oddity of coming from posh stock, the case was considerably spiced up by the fact that, following young Jonathan Goldstein's arrest, the police managed to get hold of two years' worth of his diaries.

Once sliced, Pop had to go *tout suite* to casualty to get stitched up. Mummy took him, leaving young Johnny alone at home. Pop told the stitching doctor some cock-and-bull about disturbing a burglar in the act at his home. The doctor told the Old Bill, who went round to the family home only to discover Johnny, still sitting in a mess of Pop's blood, saying damn right he'd done it, and damn shame he hadn't managed to kill the old bugger. Bill felt obliged to make the arrest, but Pop refused to give evidence, or press charges, so everyone agreed that a bit of Assessment might be useful, and a secure setting might help, just in case Johnny developed a taste for carving.

Anyway, Old Bill found J's diaries, which were most elegantly written, in beautiful stylised prose, and revealed some really chilling content.

Johnny had been thinking about, and planning, and preparing for a touch of cosmetic surgery on his Pop – namely an enforced separation of the old man from his bollocks through the use of the aforementioned bread knife. As Ken Kaminsky would've said, "Oh dearie me!" and, as Pop would doubtless have shouted, "Ouch!"

The relationship between father and son had been developing a touch of frostiness for some time. Daddy was clearly upset that his son had wanted, and indeed eventually attempted, to kill and castrate him. Jonathan was becoming increasingly annoyed that his Pop had established a longstanding habit of displaying his genitalia to his first-born, and demanding an extravagant repertoire of sex acts. So Johnny gradually developed a compelling belief that his Daddy would look so much nicer minus his bits. The whole situation was rather complicated. On the one hand, the police in possession of the diaries were inclined to the view that a charge of clearly premeditated, attempted murder was well worth a punt in Crown Court. But Daddy's implacable refusal to testify, to accept the role and responsibilities of being the acknowledged victim of this putative crime, put the mockers on that one.

Then, on the other hand, Johnny Boy himself was the victim of systematic and sustained sexual abuse at the hands of his father. This was an apparent reality which had been hauntingly chaptered and versed in the diaries. But Jonathan also stood, in the eyes of the law, as an evidential refusenik. A Mexican stand-off of mutual denial had been accomplished and forensics were unlikely to yield any evidence of substance – unless of course Jonathan had refrained from brushing his teeth, or swallowing, for quite some time.

And as for Mum, Stum! She saw, said, knew, understood, remembered, precisely nothing.

Bottom line was, the police neither wanted nor felt able to get their day – or more likely weeks on bloody end – in court. And so, it all boiled down to Beecliffe staging a wee carnival of an Assessment meeting. Dr Aveyleigh sat at the head of the conference table, centre-stage, in the big chair, the carver. Daddy and Mummy sat at the far end, Johnny Boy opposite them, twelve feet of polished oak separating the unhappy family. Along the flank there was me – the report-writer and presenter. Plus, Dr Sam Habib, forensic psychiatrist, and Dr Angela Starling, educational psychologist, increasingly well-known pundit, and, in my personal opinion, raving nutter. Sitting across from us were three well-dressed, well-heeled and, I thought, well-chosen characters. Marsha Cohen had been appointed as Johnny's guardian–ad-litem, and looked to me as if she was sitting very comfortably in Mr Goldstein's very deep pocket. Barry Feltz was senior social work lecturer from Goldsmiths College – in deepest Deptford – and said he was there "purely as an observer." And lastly, there was Chief Superintendent George Butterfield who proclaimed, with toe-curling pomposity, his "sole and simple purpose of ensuring that justice shall prevail."

First Dr Sam, then Dr Angela, delivered their "specialist reports", which were fairly brief, laden with professional jargon and substantially incomprehensible. Dr Aveyleigh revealed his class by elucidating their meaning, and then trumping their jargon with a tour-de-force of erudite opacity. This, I thought, was taking head-wanking to new and dizzy heights – an Olympic sport, and new art-form. Then it was my turn. My role was to present the Beecliffe Assessment Report, comprising pen-picture, personal history, observations at the Assessment Centre, young person's views and conclusion. For me, this had been, in a perverse kind of way, a labour of love. I had worked on it diligently for the past three weeks, and manically for the past seventy-two hours. I took pride in my creation, and delivered it with panache. Its tone and content were generally sympathetic to Jonathan, a kid with whom I felt I could identify, despite the fact that he was a kid with whom I had virtually nothing in common. The report also contained a liberal seasoning of hand-grenades, intended for and aimed at Daddy, a man for whom I harboured a visceral loathing. These bomblets were wrapped in a thin skin of feigned objectivity, but their targets and purpose were glowingly transparent.

All of that stuff took an hour and a bit. Then Dr Aveyleigh gave us an uninterrupted ten-minute soliloquy through which he proved, beyond a scintilla of doubt, how and why his was, by a long chalk, the cleverest brain in the room.

Then he did the thing with his left hand, which he raised dramatically, palm towards his face.

First, he held his little finger, between the thumb and index of his right hand. This, he announced, represented the prospect of any kind of psychiatric diagnosis. And here, the clearly established absence of any abnormality or disorder (gracious nod to Dr Sam) precluded the need for medical treatment. So the pinkie was folded, neatly and conclusively back into the palm. Next, to the ring finger, and the burgeoning world of Special Educational Needs (a mere perfunctory nod to Dr Angy). None assessed, so same result, fold down the finger. The middle finger stands for legal procedures and possible penal convictions. (A coy smile delivered to our Chief Super.) It's a no-go zone, so further finger-folding.

Now we're down to index and thumb. Mounting excitement ripples round the table, particularly for those not already familiar with the Aveyleigh hand-job. The index stands erect, and represents the range of social-services interventions. Residential homes, foster care, youth workers, counsellors. The good Doctor reveals that there's potential relevance here, lightly hinting at Foster Care, promising to return soon to this alluring prospect. The index finger touches the thumb in a brief caress. Dr Aveyleigh allows himself a fleeting, enigmatic smile. Then the thumb itself is raised, alone, affirming, positive. The thumb reveals its pleasure, which is for an expensive and very exclusive boarding school in Scotland. The thumb reminds us all that Jonathan has admitted to the assault on his father, and has shown his sincere, heartfelt remorse. Dr Aveyleigh uses his whole hand, joined quickly by his other one, to make an irresistibly imploring pair, which both extol and underpin his oratory. He proclaims that Jonathan's behaviour was the understandable enactment of extraordinary tensions and pressures – unique to the circumstances in which they were manifested. He then concludes that, by attending a good school, and being placed with supportive foster parents during holiday times, Jonathan is no more, and no less, likely to perpetrate acts of violence than anyone else sitting there in the room.

Having thus established the undisputed facts, and drawn the ineluctable conclusions, and having proved that he, Dr Aveyleigh, stands before us all as the very re-incarnation of Wise King Solomon, he asks his congregation if anyone has any alternative views or suggestions. So, to slightly paraphrase the immortal words from 'The Walrus and the Carpenter' "But answers come there none… And this was scarcely odd, because…"

The meeting is over. The masterclass is done. And now it's time for tea.

16

As the meeting was breaking up, and various pairs of hands were shaking, Dr Aveyleigh asked me to accompany him back to his office. I was surprised, and vaguely anxious. We walked into his room – the same one I'd been interviewed in the previous November, all but a year ago. He invited me to sit down and took an adjacent chair himself. With barely a pause for breath, he began. "Firstly, Jack, I want to congratulate you on a remarkable piece of writing, well done."

I felt a very warm and pleasant glow arrive in the pit of my stomach, which then gently spread through me from head to toe.

Dr Aveyleigh indulged me for the moment, and then flicked the switch with a staccato, "However!" which hung in the air. A hint of menace, certainly. Plus, perhaps a touch of malice.

"However, Jack, there is something fundamental which you have yet to learn. Something crucial to the process of writing the kind of Assessment Report that achieves the very highest standard. And this is the need to understand the difference between the use of denotative, as opposed to connotative language. Let me try to illustrate my point. If a TV weatherman were to say, 'Early morning mist may be stubbornly persistent though the strong June sun will be trying to burn it off and give us welcome warmth by the afternoon.' Such a statement conveys information about the weather but also information about the attitude of the weatherman. However, can you see how exactly the same weather might be described very differently by a different weatherman, perhaps a pale skinned hay-fever sufferer who cherishes cool cloud and a low pollen count?

"Coming back to your report, Jack, in the section relating to the parental interviews which you conducted, you say, 'The father's facial expression conveyed an impression of self-pity laced with guilt…' and, later on, 'It was as if he wanted to give vent to his emotions and indulge himself in the luxury of wallowing in an exhibitionist flood of crocodile tears'. This may well serve in the context of a romantic novel, but it is quite unacceptable as part of an Assessment Report.

"To be honest with you Jack, the nature of your achievement with this assessment report was to elicit and excite emotion. But, the true purpose of such reports is not to stir the emotions, nor yet to elucidate the preferences and prejudices of their authors. They should not be written with the aim to amuse and entertain. They must be factually accurate, coherent, and cogently argued. They must tell the truth, as far as it can be adduced, but a truth stripped to its bare essentials, without embellishment or decoration. Do you understand, Jack?"

I say, "Thank you, Dr Aveyleigh. I appreciate you taking the time to tell me all this." Though I say it through the same set of clenched teeth that imparted my appreciation for him having corrected my errant pronunciation of the superfluous 't' when I mentioned a trait during my interview.

When I got home, a couple of hours later, Fizz was immediate in her request for feedback about my first Big Deal meeting. My response was well short of the grace or warmth she deserved.

She winced, as if I had slapped her. And then she said to me, "What's happening to you Jack? You're not the same. Half of the time I feel like I don't know you anymore." That, for sure, was the raw truth, stripped of embellishment – but a truth I couldn't see or accept in that moment. So I just meanly muttered, under my breath, "Well fuck you, and fuck Dr Bastard Aveyleigh both." And I picked up my stash box, and Marley's lead, and skulked out of the door for a walk with the dog and a solo spliff.

The first half-hour of that walk was fast and absolutely furious. Normally, Marley will pull and strain on the leash, given half a chance. But this time, she just trotted along at my side, giving me repeated, anxious-looking sideways glances. As we progressed along narrowing country lanes, and then onto single-track public footpaths, the manic dimension started to ebb out of our headlong pace, and softer thoughts began to flow into my mind. The path wound up hill. Arable fields gave way to a patch of woodland, mixed, mostly deciduous, leaves beginning to turn and fall. The ground was damp, smelling strongly of autumn. We found a capsized trunk of silver birch which offered the perfect dry seat. Out with the stash box; too much wind to easily stick three papers together, so I just rolled a one-skin joint, half-and-half Old Holborn and powerful ganja. I took three consecutive deep lungfuls on first lighting it. The sure- fire sign of its potency was that it went straight to my feet and ankles. They did a little joyful dance of excited pins and needles, and then the effect worked its way up through the considerable length of my entire body till it got to my brain, whose tongue had been hanging out in rapt anticipation. I thanked sweet Jesus for the blessings of ganja, and stared, double-glazed, at the woodland carpet, all those iridescent "falling leaves, which jewel the ground, [and] know the art of dying." And that's how and when I clocked it. Five years gone, to the very day. The fifth anniversary of Nancy's funeral.

It wasn't just Fizz who didn't know what had happened to me, or who I was half the time. I didn't know either but, the problem was, until then I didn't know that I didn't know. This was the first appearance of that rather important question, and I wasn't at all sure that I liked it. And I certainly wasn't sure whether I'd like to pursue it to the point of finding any answers. But, with the helpful contribution of the spliff, which provided a comforting local anaesthetic for my fragile emotions, I was happy to do a bit of sniffing round the edges, and to make a semi-detached survey of the area.

I sensed that there was a compelling jigsaw puzzle at hand, which would ultimately reveal quite a significant big picture. But for now, I was more than happy to just pick up some individual pieces, and look at them with an isolated interest, without trying to fit bits together or force any issues. The first piece was obvious, the source of the metaphor, Nancy's funeral, staring me in the face. I dived into my memory, and re-joined the pitiful little huddle in the church. In that moment, the gut-wrenching, sickening pain was undimmed and completely undiminished. Time had not been any kind of healer, just an irrelevance. But then the picture did move on, and re-focused in our front room and settled on an evening, nearly a week after the funeral. My Ma and Step Pa had left the day before, with Step Pa not quite saying it out loud, but clearly demonstrating his belief in, and adherence to, his pungent little Chinese proverb, the one that goes "Guests, like fish, start to stink after three days."

It was the first evening we'd had to ourselves, and Fizz had put Flo to bed, still in our room, but no longer needing her mother's uninterrupted night-time vigil – just repeated and regular checking. We were between checks and Fizz said, "How long do you think it can last?" and I said, "What last?" and she said, "This silence with Flo. This state of petrified shock she seems to be stuck in." I said that I had no idea, but that I was sure she'd be OK, and that all she needed was to know that we love her and will carry on looking after her, and will just treat her absolutely as normal, as if nothing has happened. And Fizz said, "Maybe she needs professional help. Maybe she should see a child psychologist, or a doctor or someone."

All I can see in my mind is an army of White Coats. And all I can say is, "No way!" And the sum total of reply from Fizz was, "I'm going to check her again. Then I think I'll stay up there."

Next to that jigsaw piece, lying face down on the leaf-jewelled woodland floor, was another, which caught my eye. I picked it up and turned it over in my hand. It was an illustrated inscription, beautiful copperplate handwriting, surrounded by elegant twirls in gold leaf. "Least said, soonest mended." It was a piece of my Ma.

I was nearly ready to go home, and Marley had plainly had enough of sitting in one spot. I scooped up all the remaining, yet-to-be-examined jigsaw pieces, popped them into the box, and secured the lid tight shut. Ready for off. The melody of The String Band's October song was playing in my head, rich and strong. Then the lyrics of the last verse arrived, and I belted them out, full throttle.

> "Sometimes I'd like to murder time
> Sometimes when my heart is breaking
> But mostly, I just drift along
> The path that he is making."

I picked up two of the nicest and brightest leaves to take home. One was for Fizz, the other for Flo.

As Marley and I walked back into the house, I could hear Fizz singing. There hadn't been much of that for quite some time, and I'd almost forgotten just how gorgeous her voice is – somewhere between Ella at her most soulful and Roberta Flack at her most haunting. I left Marley in the kitchen, noisily and messily downing a bowlful of water. I went into the lounge, where Fizz was sitting in the armchair, cradling Flo in her arms. Fizz finished off the last couple of lines – a song I didn't recognise – and then stopped. I said, to both of them, "I'm sorry. I didn't mean to disturb you," and Fizz said, "It's OK. Anyway, I was just about to go to the kitchen to start cooking our tea. Why don't you stay here with Flo, and play something on the stereo – something which you'll both like." And then I said, just to Fizz, "I'm so sorry about earlier. I know I've been really uptight for days, over this stupid bloody Big Deal Report business, and straight after the meeting, Dr Aveyleigh took me into his office, and started off by giving me a bit of a glowing compliment, then followed it by a slow-burn bollocking which made me feel humiliated, although it was seriously true and well-deserved. I'd just soaked up all that stuff and then I spat the venom at you, and you didn't deserve it." After a pause for a couple of shaky breaths, I went on.

"Anyway, I brought you and Flo each a present from the pretty woods." Flo took her leaf in silence, gave it a cursory glance, looked away, but held on to it. Fizz took hers, and said it was beautiful and amazing, and that she would dry and press and treasure it. Then I said to Fizz, "Do you know what day it is today, what anniversary?" And she told me of course she did, but she hadn't dared to say anything, so I said I thought we should talk, properly, after Flo's gone to bed, and Fizz said, "Sure." And we both said, in near-perfect unison, "About bloody time."

Fizz went into the kitchen without closing the lounge door, and said to Marley, "Hello, you beautiful black bitch. Just look at the wet mess you've made all over my clean kitchen floor, you great trollop." Then she started singing again, the same song I'd interrupted earlier.

I was really happy to hear Fizz singing, but more than that, I felt something like an urgent need to listen again to the String Band's October song. I found the album – The Five Thousand Layers or the Spirits of the Onion – then I turned to Flo who was lying on the sofa, one leg dangling over the side, and I said to her, "We played this song at Nancy's funeral, and it's the anniversary today."

No discernible reaction.

I went straight to the track, played it through and pressed "eject" the moment it finished. My cheeks were just slightly tear-stained, but otherwise I thought I probably looked pretty normal. But little Flo gave me a piercing stare, and said, quite clearly, "Poor Daddy. Nanny gone now. Nanny gone." and I said, "Yes darling, that's right, she is. And we all miss her terribly."

Then she said, "Yes, poor little Flo."

17

Of course, it's not exactly like I've said. Little Flo hasn't been a constantly immobile, absolutely silent mute, from the very moment her sister gave up the ghost. The reality is, she does move about a bit, she does make sounds every so often, even says the occasional word. And in fact, when she's asleep she gives every appearance of having vivid, active dreams. A bit like Marley when she's snoring away and looks for all the world as if she's running hell-for-leather after rabbits across the moors. There are bits that Flo says and does, but they all seem pretty disconnected and remote. It's as if her moments of activity or engagement slip out unawares, and then as soon as she notices, the shutters crash down again, the defences regain control, the lights go back out.

I can't remember now, exactly when we first saw the pictures of those Romanian orphanage babies on TV. I think that it must have been some time much later on. But I do remember, with a horrible pang, how Fizz and I saw them together, and said, together, "Oh my God," because we had clocked, "Just like Flo used to look." Haunted, and remote, and removed from her spontaneous connection with life.

But anyway, when she actually spoke and conveyed relevant meaning, on the fifth anniversary of Nancy's funeral, that was an absolute shock. And it was pure bliss. A whopping great milestone for Flo, me and, later, Fizz. And I did realise, more or less straight away, that her words came after my mention of the funeral and Nancy by name. It was my first breach of the great taboo. Unbelievable! How could I possibly have thought that my total censorship of Nancy could have been helpful and supportive to Little Flo? Ridiculous! But, at that time I hadn't heard the essential joke about denial being more than just a river in Egypt.

After tea, one of our all-time favourites, fish fingers, chips and beans followed by syrup sponge and custard, Fizz said that she fancied going for a walk with the pooch, and could I do the honours of bath-and-bed routine with Flo, and I happily said, "It's a deal."

We did the bath with the bubbles, and I played with the ducks and the little clockwork toy of the black girl in a polka-dot bikini who did the backstroke for half the length of the tub. Flo watched her, smiled a bit, and said, "Again" a few times. Which was not exactly unique, but it was unusual.

After we'd done the routine of towel-down, hair-dry and skin-creaming, which made her glow like honey in sunshine, I took out the Children's Anthology of Poems, and read 'The Walrus and the Carpenter', mostly because it's one of my favourites. Flo just lay there, pretty unresponsive throughout, but she seemed to be a touch more relaxed, as if she had slightly loosened the grip on her usually tight-clenched shell. Once the poor little oysters had been eaten, every one, I put the book away, but made no move to go. Usually, end of story equals end of everything – kiss on the forehead, lights out, gone.

But now, I don't want to go anywhere. I'm staying put.

After a few minutes, we hear the front door open downstairs, hear Mummy taking off her wellies, hear Marley giving herself a shake and then the click click click of her nails as she walks across the kitchen lino, swiftly followed by the metallic clank of her collar against her water bowl as she slurps away. All soothing, safe and familiar.

Little Flo's eyes are closed, but I know she's not asleep. So, to my own surprise and astonishing relief, I start to tell her. All of it. How much I miss Nancy, how afraid I'd been to even say her name out loud, how I'd thought it would only make Mummy, and Flo herself, even more upset if we talked about Nancy, and how wrong that all feels now. I become aware that Fizz is standing just inside the door, a couple of feet away from me. But I carry on anyway, and say that I've just started to think that talking about our hurts actually eases the pain, if only we can find the courage to do it. Fizz gives a big sigh, and says "A'right."

And little Flo opens her eyes, and says, "I'm sorry Nanny,

I didn't mean it", and then closes her eyes, roles onto her side, and holds Ted close to her neck. Within a minute, she's fast asleep. And it seems to us as if she's at peace, genuinely and completely at peace, for the first time since Nancy's been gone.

Fizz and I go downstairs together, into the sitting room, give Marley the look, and ask her how dare she, as we shove her off the sofa, then settle down at either end of it. I've got Fizz's feet in my lap, and start with toe-pulling – prelude to the massage routine. I ask her, "How was your walk with Marls?" and she says it was fine, and that she'd had a good cry for Nancy, and had thought she'd better do that whilst giving Flo, and more particularly me, a wide berth, but now she's wondering if she'd really needed to. I give her my best impersonation of a Jamaican "Mmm", to which she replies with an authentic "Yeah Mon."

And as I'm massaging the left foot, I begin to tell her about my walk with Marley, starting at the point of arrival at the birch bench, and the rolling of the spliff. I ask if she fancies one now, and she tells me maybe later, and to just keep talking for the moment. So I do, telling her about the prompt of the falling leaves, the remembrance of October Song, the discovery of the jigsaw puzzle lying in bits amongst the leaves, with the first piece standing for the funeral, and the second one, my Ma's mantra of "Least said, soonest mended." I say that when I found this piece, I remembered one of my psychology lectures at university – an introduction to Gestalt. The professor, a nice cuddly old grandma who I'd always liked, gave us the word "introjects" and said that, "We acquire them, imbided like our mother's milk, and they become part of our very essence, our DNA, unquestioned, unless, through an effort of conscious will, we take them out for considered examination." Then she invited us to spend ten minutes, working with the person sitting next to us, dredging up some of these introjects, giving them a good inspection, and then seeing what we consciously think about them. So, the one I found was my Ma saying, "Come on now, Jack, don't make a fuss!" which, I started to realise, boils down to, "Don't say what you feel – at least if you're feeling upset or angry or, God forbid, anguished. Better, by far, to bottle it up!"

So, there and then, as the psychology student, I had felt like I could recognise some of that stuff, but I was still somehow distanced from it. But this afternoon, I had picked up one of the jigsaw pieces, and I knew straight away that it was Ma's, and the quote was, "Least said, soonest mended." That one went through me like a stiletto, and it's left me feeling a bit sick. Then I thought a moment, and said, "No, that's not quite it. It's not feeling a bit sick, its feeling like I've just *been* sick, like I've puked up a little clot of something which was poisonous. And now, although I'm shaky, I'm actually feeling a whole lot better."

I talk, on and on. Fizz offers occasional words of encouragement, and later a pot of tea and a packet of fig rolls. But we don't bother with the spliff.

Much, much later, we go to bed. This time, at the same time. Usually Fizz goes up by herself, at least a couple of hours before me. But not tonight. When we go into the bedroom, we can both tell that Little Flo is OK, without any need to do elaborate checking. Fizz gets into her side of the bed, on the left, after squeezing through the narrow gap separating our double from Flo's slim size single. She removes one of her two pillows, dropping it on the floor.

I hear Marley, softly padding up the carpeted stairs, up to the landing and doing her routine of turning round a couple of times before she lies down, loosely coiled, her head propped on her own cushion of rear leg and tail. She heaves a mighty sigh and is comfortably snoring within a minute.

I open the top window a notch and draw back the curtains, a little either side of it. The wind has dropped, almost to nothing. There's a line of thin cloud, retreating from mid sky towards the western horizon. The moon, at first just a vague patch of silvery brightness, emerges into sharply defined clarity.

Cool air touches me from head to toe, giving me goose bumps running up my arms to the back of my neck. It feels refreshing and cleansing, like washing off salt and sand after a day at the beach. Fizz says, "Jack, come into bed and warm me up. I'm chilly in here," and I tell her I will, in a minute.

My head feels awash with memories, all of which seem to be sparkling with a freshly polished vibrancy. And each one appears not only to be revitalised in its own right, but also hungry to connect and communicate with its neighbours. An imposed censorship is lifting, whilst light begins to flood into the centre of my being, which had, literally, been kept in the dark for the whole time since I had wrapped and covered the open sore of bereavement with that emergency dressing.

I look down at my chest and belly, and I notice, for the first time, that the enormous sticking plaster I've been wearing for so many years is starting to lift away, at the bottom edge. My immediate impulse is to try to stick it back down, or to find a new bit to stick over it, to patch over the patch. But then I think, no, maybe not. Maybe I should try to lift it a bit, take a peep inside, find out what's going on down there.

Fizz says "Jack?" Sounding like she's half-asleep. I climb into bed, and as we touch, she gives out a little shriek of "Ow, brrrr… you're freezing." She doesn't flinch or pull away, but takes my right hand in hers, and kisses my fingertips, then holds it around her breast. Just before falling asleep, she murmurs, "Tomorrow, I'm going to move Flo's bed into her own room. It's time."

Then, slowly and gently, we sink down together from the surface of our perceptions to the bottomless depths of rest, and a peace which knows nothing of separation, a peace which passes all understanding.

18

Looking back now at that time in Beecliffe, those Big Deal Assessment Reviews certainly stick in the mind. It's natural, for incidents of spectacular and often horrific crimes, committed by children, some of whom were barely into their teenage years, it's natural for that stuff to stick out in the filing cabinets of memory lane. But the fact is that there's one recollection I have, one which I remember more clearly, and was touched by more deeply, than all the murders, rapes, arsons and attempted suicides put together. And it probably exerted a greater influence on me wanting to, and actually staying in that line of business for the following thirty odd years.

I'd been working in the Secure Assessment Unit for a couple of years, and had been appointed as its "Manager and Team Leader" nine months or so earlier.

It was about ten in the evening. I was at home, but was also the On Call Duty Manager. The internal phone rang. "Hi, Jack. We've got an emergency admission coming to the secure unit. Police are bringing her in. Not much info yet. They're coming from Newcastle. Said they should be here in half-an-hour. Can you get yourself up here, and get a single bedroom ready. I'll tell you more as soon as I know it." This was from Terry Ramsden, one of the night care officers, ex-army, semi-retired.

Fizz had just gone upstairs, but wasn't yet asleep. So I let her know the score, picked up my keys, told Marley not to get herself excited for nothing, and quietly closed the front door behind me. Three minutes later, I was sitting at my desk in the secure unit's office, and one minute after that, Terry joined me. He made tea for both of us, which we drank from the stained and grimy plastic mugs that we used up there. No china, no glass, no metal. All too risky. Terry said, "I've had a bit of a chat with the custody sergeant from the nick in Wallsend. They didn't want to keep her in the cells. They think the lass is only about thirteen or so. Neighbours called the police. Apparently there was a right bloody row. Kitchen smashed to bits. Blood and mess all over the place. The Mam had some deep cuts, and it looks like it was the bairn that done it. Mam went off in an ambulance, and she's under sedation whilst she's getting herself sewn together again. They think she'll live OK but maybe's she'll not look the same. That's about as much as he could tell us."

I try a couple of sips of tea but can only taste the plastic. I take a deep breath. "Right then. Are you here for the whole night, Terry?" He says he'll probably swap with Barry who's covering the non-secure units, but only if everything's quiet. I say, "Talking of quiet, are all our lot settled? Do you think any of them could've caught wind of our imminent arrival?" But Terry thinks they've not caught a sniff, and we should be OK.

Louise is my member of sleeping-in staff tonight. She's in the common room, the other end of the corridor at the moment, writing up the daily observation sheets. I walk down to join her, tell her the score, and ask her to come back with me to the office while we await the Old Bill, and our young guest's arrival.

I thank God, and my lucky stars, that Louise is on sleep-in duty tonight. Virtually without exception, all the kids love her. And not only that. They love her immediately. She's not a slowly acquired taste.

I know hardly anything about her really. She's been working at Beecliffe for a few months, and before that, worked in some residential unit in Liverpool. She's a Scouser, as broad as they come. She's blonde, big, buxom, has very white teeth and very black mascara, laid on thick. She smiles a lot and laughs infectiously. She doesn't scare easily and generally, at the first sign of potential trouble, she'll say, "No. Surely not. I can't believe that...!" And as soon as the potential trouble sees what it's up against, it just tends to slink off in search of a likelier customer or softer target.

All of which makes me feel really happy that she's sitting next to me as we spot the blue flashing light pulling up in the parking bay below.

I tell Terry to hold the fort while Louise and I go downstairs to greet the Old Bill and our new arrival.

Two large Geordies are standing outside the van, both having a fag. I know one of them from previous business, and he gives me a curt nod and a not very friendly, "OK, Jack?" After another deep pull on his fag, which he then drops to the ground and extinguishes with a big black boot, he says, "We've got her in the back. She's secured to the floor. Fucking wild she is, man, I'm telling yer." Then, his mate, if anything the meaner and nastier of the pair, says, "We'll escort her upstairs and into the unit. Once she's in, you sign for her, then you're responsible for her, OK?" I tell them that I understand the procedure. Mean one looks at nasty one and says, "Come on then, let's get shot of her." Louise looks at me, shakes her head, and mutters, "Sweet Jesus" under her breath.

As they open the back doors of the van, one dim little light illuminates the sad and very sorry scene. A powerful and repugnant stench rolls out. She's laying there, hands tightly cuffed behind her back, a short length of thick metal chain attaching her to an even thicker metal ring which is welded to the floor. Our view is obscured by the two beefy officers, but we are able to make out that they treat her with a mixture of brutality and distain, dragging her roughly, backwards out of the van, then keeping the pressure on, against the elbow joints, painfully forcing her head down, hauling her up the stairs. In the office, the bigger one removes the paperwork from his breast pocket, tells me where to sign, twice, leaves the carbon copy, and says, "Right", before unlocking the cuffs. I say, "Louise, can you show the officers out, please," and she says, "No, you're all right. You do that, while I take care of Young Precious." And the big one says, "Aye, Precious, she's that all right," and Precious clears her throat, and prepares to spit straight in his face, but Louise gets herself between them and says to her, "You're OK, love, you'll be safe with us. Nothing and nobody is going to hurt you now." And we all believe her, there and then, on that spot. The power of conviction. Awesome.

I walk with the Old Bill to their van. They're talking between themselves, about the "fucking crazy half-caste bitch." I try to ask one or two straight-forward questions, but get only prejudice and derision back from them, so I just turn on my heel to go back upstairs. I'm feeling that I've behaved like a coward, that I should have somehow challenged them, but I fob off my conscience with a quick and dismissive, "What's the point?"

When I walk back into the office, there's no sign of Precious, or Louise, but Terry is sitting there, and he tells me that "Lou's taken the bairn for a bath. The poor lass bloody well needs one." I make a start on the paperwork – the basics, date and time of admission, legal status; date of birth etc, and then I start to wonder, just a bit, about the person to whom these facts and figures relate, and the quirks of fate and fortune which have brought her here tonight.

After about a quarter of an hour, Louise pokes her head round the office door. "Right, she's bathed and beautified now. But I think the poor kid hasn't got a clue about where she is or what's happening. Do you want to have a word?" And I tell her, "Sure, but you come and join me." So, we pop in to Precious's bedroom, and find her sitting on her bed, wrapped up in the duvet, hugging her knees and rocking back and forth. She doesn't look at me, but does glance, briefly and repeatedly at Louise, who sits on the end of the bed while I sit down on the floor, opposite the pair of them. Precious looks up, vaguely in my direction, then more specifically, at my size fourteen feet.

And then I think I get it, from her point of view. How could she possibly know whether or not I'm one of the white-coat types, about to launch into a pile of nasty invasive questions. So I say to her, "Precious, later on, we will talk. There are lots of questions I want to ask you, but they can wait. For the moment, if you have any questions, you can ask me, or ask Louise. But the really important thing I want to say right now is the same as what Louise has already said. You'll be safe here. Nobody is going to hurt you. We promise."

And Louise says, directly to her, "Listen to me, Precious, you don't have to worry about him, love. I know he's enormous, and he looks peculiar, and he's got that funny eye, and those hands. But he's alright, really he is." Precious seems to take what Louise says with a pinch of salt, and keeps a tight hold on her knees, and keeps her own counsel, and keeps her gaze pretty much fixed on the floor. We sit for a bit. I heave a great sigh. Lou does likewise, and, for good measure adds, "Jesus, what a bloody night. Does anyone fancy a cupper and a digestive?" Precious says, after a short pause, "Water. Just water, please."

Her "water" breaks the ice, and melts her silence.

19

In terms of sudden, absolutely unexpected shocks, I'd have to rate this one as an all-time winner. Today is Thursday 14th April. Dawn broke with no fanfare of trumpet and bright lights, just a gradual evolution from pitch black to dank and drizzling grey. I was there to see it, as I'd been up since 4.30. The alarm had dragged me out of bed, because I had at least three hours work to do, in order to complete my current Big Deal Assessment Report. I'd finished the pen picture, observations and child's view sections pretty much, though I wanted to give myself a re-visit and edit option. But I hadn't done the conclusion, and this one was causing me serious head-scratching consternation.

There were probably seven or eight reports which stood in between Jonathan G's and this one. Some had been fairly run-of-the-mill, a couple with standout features.

I had been trying, consciously, to take on board what Dr Aveyleigh had said to me about using denotative language, and had actually become quite intrigued with the challenge, and the process. Some seriously interesting questions had arisen. Like, is it really possible to describe another person's behaviour objectively? Is there such a thing as a detached description of the motivation underpinning an action? Can we actually make an assessment which is free of value judgement? Does the act of looking at something in itself change what we see? All this stuff makes for interesting musing, but doesn't actually help getting the report done to deadline. And this one, for sure, has a deadline. Namely 10 o'clock this morning. Absolutely must be done and dusted, to be read out loud to the meeting, with no ad-hocking or ad-libbing, and then ready to hand in for typing the moment the meeting ends.

This meeting will be a whopper. At least a dozen round the conference table. The entourage will include folk with big titles, and lots of letters after their names. Folk who, between them, hold, to a significant degree, the fate and future of one particular young person, Grace, in their collective hands.

The basic facts are beyond dispute. Two adults, one of whom was extremely drunk, were engaged in a violent argument. The latest episode in a long series. The argument took place in their kitchen. The kitchen in a remote hillside farmhouse. The shotgun was on the wall. It was loaded. The sixteen-year-old girl pulled the trigger. The shot removed most of her stepdad's face, lots of his neck and, within about ten minutes, the last of his life. That's why she had been remanded to the care of the Local Authority and placed in the Secure Unit at Beecliffe to undergo a six-week residential assessment. The Assessment Reports would comprise, along with the expert witness testimony of their authors, essential ingredients in the forthcoming Crown Court trial.

So, Big Deal for sure. And for me, it provided a big opportunity to try to get my contribution as right as I possibly could, not just in content, but in tone.

I had appointed myself as keyworker and report writer for Grace, the day she was admitted to the centre.

And to cap it all, the whole Assessment Review meeting was going to be videoed for later use as staff training material.

After another three hours of intense work, I had it done by about half-past seven. I read it out loud, making the odd minor adjustment whenever I found a bit that didn't quite sound as I wanted it to. I could hear Fizz and Flo upstairs, getting themselves up and ready for the day, and as I finished the final paragraph, and said, "Done it," Marley did her stretch-yawn-and-shake number, and invited me to join her for a walk. I was happy to oblige, and the walk turned into a run, the three-mile circuit round the back of the centre and on to the Beecliffe village loop. We got back, twenty-five minutes later, panting, mud-flecked and knackered.

Fizz asked me what I wanted for breakfast as I was on my way up for a shower, and I told her that a mere half-a-horse would do nicely.

At quarter to ten, I was there in the conference room, my report safe and snug inside my briefcase, with my brogues polished to a high glossy shine, wearing my newish Pierre Cardin pinstripe, bought in the January sales, freshly removed from its dry cleaner's bag, a brand-new crimson shirt, a silver tie, my hair and beard shampooed and conditioned. I was done to a T, and smelled powerfully of my Christmas present cologne. My nerves were definitely jangling, but I was feeling well up for it, waiting for the whistle, raring to go.

I'd seen a little gaggle of them gathering in Dr Aveyleigh's room but hadn't clocked any faces in particular. At ten o'clock on the nose, he led them all into the conference room, where I'd been waiting, at first on my own, then with Ed Macklusky, the training officer, who was busy setting up the video stuff.

Dr Aveyleigh was taking absolute control from the outset, directing people to their seats like a head waiter at a banquet. I already knew my place, second to the left of the boss himself. So, I'd just started to actually take notice of individual faces, when I saw her, and simultaneously heard him, saying "Doctor Mandrake, please will you sit here next to me, and beside Jack Warren, our report writer. Let me introduce you."

I flushed, immediately, matching the colour of my shirt. I mumbled something incomprehensible, and dashed out of the room, down the corridor, into the toilet, into a cubicle and locked the door. This, in itself, turned out to be the perfect place of good fortune, as I had then to immediately separate myself from the large breakfast of ninety minutes ago, which had somehow completed its journey from stomach to sphincter, and

130

demanded to get outside me. Once I was empty, I just sat there, pants and trousers round the ankles, shivering, shaking and softly whimpering. After a few deep breaths, the sense of blind panic started to abate. I gradually began to realise that, although I hadn't seen Dr M since I was her patient in the Adolescent Psychiatric Unit, the fact of seeing her again here did not re-place me in that previous context. Dr M's purpose in being here was not to assess me, it was to participate in the review meeting being held for Grace. I told myself that I would, and it would, all be fine. So I wiped and sorted myself, came out of the cubicle, washed my hands, straightened my tie, and started the walk back towards the conference room. The whole mini-drama had probably lasted no more than two or three minutes.

As I passed the ladies toilets, with impeccable timing, Dr M emerged. She looked me squarely in the eye, and said, "I think that Dr Aveyleigh was just about to introduce us. He has told me a little about you and the work you've been doing here. He seems to have great confidence in you." And she gives me her hand – just as warm and comforting as I had remembered it. And I know that she knows, absolutely, who I am, and how we were previously brought together. And the slight inflection which she gives to the word "confidence" reassures me that the nature of our previous relationship is absolutely safe and securely protected. We walk towards the conference room together, and as we approach the door, she says, "Now, let's see what we can discover of the truth about young Grace's situation." And I say to her, "Yes absolutely, it's what we're all here for."

*

131

After the meeting, I bumped into Dr M in the car park. She had spent half-an-hour ensconced with Dr Aveyleigh in his office. I'd popped home for a short tea break, and to exchange my suit for my more normal, casual workwear. Fizz was due to go into Darlington for some shopping plus a hairdresser's appointment. Flo was due to visit with Martina and Louis, a couple of kids who had taken a shine to her, and whose mum had become best mates with Fizz. I'd offered to walk Flo across on my way back to work.

Dr Aveyleigh had escorted Dr M to her car. They were just saying their goodbyes as Flo and I came in sight.

Dr M said hello directly to Flo, who looked at her without any kind of reaction or response. Par for Flo with a stranger. I felt a bit awkward, but unable to get into any kind of excuse or explanation for Flo's apparent bad manners. Dr M had definitely tuned-in to the atmosphere, and managed to defuse it by saying that she herself often feels uncomfortable when she meets someone for the first time, and finds it difficult to know quite what to say. So, we're off the hook. Then Dr M focused on me, and said, "I've just been having a discussion with Dr Aveyleigh. He's asked me if I will be able to do some assessment work with young people here, and also some staff training and I've agreed, to both." I told her that I'm really delighted to hear this news, and that I hoped to be able to attend the training. Then I asked her if it was not going to be a long trek coming all the way from London, and she told me no, because she's now based in Newcastle, where her main job was launching a research project on the effects of traumatic shock on children and young adults. And I said, "Really, now that's something I'd definitely like to know more about." And she said, "I'm glad to hear that, and you certainly will."

With that, and with mutual look-forward-to-seeing-you-soons, we went our separate ways.

20

Fizz

I don't think Jack had ever wanted to keep it a secret, his "Teenage time banged up with the nutters," as he called it. In fact, he made a point of mentioning it pretty soon after we met. He said something along the lines of, "Before you get too involved with me, you need to know that I used to be crazy. Officially. Certified. But that was when I was an understandably-fucked-up teenager. However, now, I don't believe that I need to have any psychiatrists, counsellors or prescription drugs to keep me safe and sane." Then one of his pointed pauses before saying, "Just loads of grade 'A' ganja." And given he had the best part of a kilo of the stuff at the time, that didn't seem too big a problem. But it felt like he'd tried to open and close the subject, all in one breath. Certainly, I didn't feel as if I'd been invited to ask questions, or encouraged to chat about that stuff. Bits and pieces have leaked out over the years, like his opinion on the White Coats, who I think he sees as a whole separate species of un-humans. And whenever he has talked about his hatred for the world of psychs, he has always, always said, "Apart from one. There was one of them who literally saved my life." And honestly, he just melts on the spot – from Mr Angry, rock-hard iceman to soppy pup – just as soon as he mentions his beloved Dr M.

So today he comes in, just before one o'clock, looking halfway between sheepish and beaming, and says, "You just won't believe this. Who I've just met, and spent the past two-and-a-bit hours with." And I say, "No, I won't. But tell me anyway." And he says, "No, not till tonight. This is a definite sit down, roll a spliff, tell you, roll another and talk about it situation." I say, "You look like you're pleased about whoever it is." And he says, "Yes, I think I am. But honestly, the minute I first saw her, I thought I was going to crap myself on the spot. And very nearly did."

At first, all I can think is that some ex-girlfriend or secret lover has suddenly turned up, and I certainly don't feel half as thrilled as he looks. He goes bounding up the stairs, three at a time, saying, "Gotta get changed and back to work in ten minutes. I'll drop Flo off on the way." And I jump to conclusions. That he's literally running away from me, trying to get off the subject, or buy himself thinking time, or just avoid having to look me in the eye. I'm standing on the bottom stair, and I yell at him, "Jack, tell me, now." So he sticks his great big daft head over the banister, and he does look me straight in the eye, and says, "It's Dr M," and I say, "Oh", then mutter, under my breath, "Thank God for that then." And then I say out loud, "Come on Flo, Daddy's going to take you round to Louis and Martina's to play for the afternoon, whilst Mummy gets her locks seen to." And Flo actually says, to my shock and joy, "Yes, I know Mummy, I'm ready already."

I got back home at five, hair done, small plaits with a few beads, having collected Flo and had a quick cuppa with Janey and her two, on the way. Jack was supposed to be off-duty himself at five, but rang on the internal phone at half-past, saying that there was a touch of trouble and strife going on which he was going to try to sort, and hoped to be home in another hour or so. In fact, the "or so" turned into a full extra three hours, and it was nearly half-nine with Flo well gone to bed, and me well on my way, when he rolled in.

"Right. I think, please God, they're settled. And for sure, thank God, I'm not on call tonight, so it's here and now beer and spliff time. You up for either?" And I said, "Definitely, both. You roll, I'll pour."

Whilst I took a couple of beers from the fridge, I asked Jack if he was hungry, and he said, "Not yet, had something indescribable on the unit. I'll wait for the munchies later."

In five minutes, we were settled on the sofa, and Jack has put on some Bach – Brandenburgs I think – and I'd poured two glasses, plus cashews and a packet of salt and vinegar crisps and I was ready. He lit the joint, took a couple of hefty pulls, licked and arrested the faster-burning side and, unusually, handed it straight to me. He kicked off with, "Well, un-be-fucking-lieveable", and told me the high drama of the conference room introduction, then the blushing pantomime of his panicky headlong dash into the loo, then the effort of will it took for him to go back to the meeting as an adult and not some "whingeing half-baked semblance of a teenage fuck-nut." He said that Dr M had cornered and collared him in the corridor and had managed to put his mind at ease. And that, once they got on with the Assessment Review, he'd felt OK – even allowing for the fact that the whole thing was being videoed. He went on, giving more snippets, about the meeting, but in fact my mind had gone off a bit then, and instead of really listening. I was just wondering what it could have been like for Dr M, watching one of her ex-patients delivering an Assessment Report about someone who is now the same age, more or less, as Jack was then.

He saw that I was glazed and drifting, and said, "Anyway, all the stuff at the meeting, that's not even half of it. When I saw you at lunchtime, I was still in a kind of excited shock with the trauma-drama of bumping into someone from a previous lifetime. It was as if my Dad suddenly rose up from his scattered ashes to say, 'Hi Jack, just thought I'd pop round to see how you're doing.' Anyway, when I was walking through the car park with Flo, I bumped into her, Dr M, again. And she told me that she's going to be coming to Beecliffe regularly, to do some forensic work with the kids here. And to do some staff training, so I said to her, 'That's a fair old trek from London' and she said, 'No, not at all, I'm based in Newcastle now. I've just started to do a research project on the effects of severe trauma on kids,' and I said, 'That's definitely something I want to hear more about', and she said, 'You will.'"

When he was telling me that entire bit, Jack had my absolute, undivided attention. No glazing or drifting off then. We both simply knew that this was huge. Just knew it. And although neither of us had started to believe in angels at that point in our lives, we both realised, quite clearly, that we'd just been blessed by one. First, and instantly, came the whole sense of realisation. Then, more slowly and gradually, as Jack said later, "We found the words to give it shape and substance."

There had never been the slightest doubt in my mind that Little Flo had gone into a state of shock ever since Nancy's death. She had been instantly transformed into an entirely different kid. The lights had gone out. Everything was locked tight shut. She seemed to be on constant look-out, in a kind of exhausted vigil, and at the same time, all her reactions were held back, or swallowed down before they could escape from her mouth. It was agony to watch. And I just longed for her to have some professional help to get better. And sometimes, I said so to Jack, pleaded with him, but he was always so sure in his reply, "Fizz, you don't know about these psychs, not from personal experience. Not like I do. If they get their hooks in, they won't let go. They'll cut you up into tiny bits so they can fit you into their neat, nasty little boxes. They've got their theories, and they'll do whatever it takes to make you fit into them. They lose sight of people and replace them with a bunch of fucking schemes and paradigms. I can't risk letting them anywhere near Little Flo. The thought just terrifies me."

How could I argue with that? How could I say, "No Jack, you're wrong there. I know better." Well, I just couldn't. What

I did say, once or twice, was, "They're not ALL the same, Jack. You know that. You say it yourself. You always bring up the fact that there was The One who saved you." And he says, "Exactly. The One. I don't mean The Few or The Occasional or The Rare Example. I mean it absolutely, literally THE ONE."

Well, he's just had a chat with The One, in the car park, and The One's told him that she's doing research on kids who've suffered trauma, and if that's not my Little Flo, then I'll be a monkey's uncle.

21

It must have been just gone midnight. Fizz and I had finished the beers in the fridge, and thank God there'd only been three or four of them. Definitely, if there'd been a dozen, I would have been on the eleventh, or last, by then. Day off to-morrow, sleep in late, recover slowly, that, without a doubt, would have been my menu of choice. But the available à la carte only provided me with lightly pissed, pretty stoned, and full to the brim with happy memories and warmly expectant fantasies about the recently re-appeared Dr M.

Fizz had just gone to bed with an indulgent but nonetheless serious health warning of, "You may not have to get up early in the morning, but Flo and I do, so I'm off now. And don't stay up all night smoking yourself crazy." And I said, "Certainly not," and I thought, I've definitely got the go-ahead for one more joint, maybe two. I'd just had the first optional extra, all to myself, big fat one, and was thinking, "Right, headphones, Hendrix." That was the exact moment the phone rang. I thought, bollocks, one of the night care staff's looking at the wrong rota. I shuffled from the sofa into the hall and picked up the receiver. It was Terry. "Hello Jack. I know you're not on duty, but it's Grace. She just won't settle. She's been ringing her buzzer every two minutes since ten o'clock. She says she's got to talk to you. And only you. Louise has been in with her, and even she can't calm or settle the bairn down. The other kids are getting wound up with the bastard buzzer now, and Grace has already said if I turn it off, she'll just start kicking the door and screaming. She says it's to do with the meeting today. Louise said I should ring you. What do you think?" What I thought was 'Oh fuck'. But what I said to Terry was, "Five minutes. Tell her I'll be there in five minutes. That's a promise. But tell her to lay off the buzzer right now." Terry said, "Right-o, Jack. Thanks."

I go up to our room, as quick and quiet as I can manage, but Fizz is already sitting up in bed, having been woken by the phone. She's turned her bedside lamp on. "So, what's up? You're not even on duty, Jack." And I tell her I know, but that I have to go anyway. She's not happy, and says so. Says stuff about her and Flo needing me, and that work is just a job but family is different, and I say, harsh and hard, "I know that," and she says, "Maybe you do know, but you don't act like you know it," and I say, "Not now. I'm going." And she says, "Go then" and turns the light out. And I'm standing, silent in the dark.

I walk out of the bedroom, and manage, just, to close the door without slamming it. I have a quick pee, rinse my mouth with a great gob full of Listerine, douse my head with cold water, squirt a couple of blasts of Old Spice and I'm off.

As I walk into the unit, Louise is there to greet me at the top of the corridor. "Hi, Jack. God, you smell nice. Are you sure you're sober enough to be here?" I tell her, "Absolutely, only had a couple left in the fridge", and she says, "Thank heavens for that then. Anyway, not a peep from herself since I said you were on your way." I say to Louise that I'll go in and talk to Grace by myself, but that I want her or Terry to do recorded checks through the spy hole, every two minutes. I go into Grace's room. It's one of the singles; we've got two four-bedded dorms, but we only ever use them for the boys. The girls always have singles. Apparently, they tried having girls share a couple of years ago. It was a bloody disaster. Literally. So, singles-only since.

The room is just big enough for the solid built-in bed frame, topped by its plastic-covered mattress. Sheet on the bottom, one thin pillow, mean and skinny duvet. Plus built-in open-fronted cupboard with two shelves. Trainers on the bottom. One change of clean clothes on the top. Nothing on the walls, which are covered in a thin layer of plastic-coated foam stuff. Dim recessed light in the ceiling. One small window, the top part of which opens about an inch, all flush to the wall. No sharp edges anywhere, no exposed screw-heads, hooks, knobs, handles. What's unusual about Grace's room, since she's been in it, is the smell. It's normal, neutral. Most of them smell of pee, adolescent sweat and manky trainers. Hers is a nice change. I go in. "Hi, Grace. They've told me you say you need to talk to me. But before we start, a couple of things I need to say to you. First, I will talk with you now. Just me. Nobody else has to be in with us. But Louise and Terry will check us, every couple of minutes, by looking through the spy hole. OK?" She gives me a nod. I go on, "Second, I've got no idea what you want to say, but whatever it is, I can't give you any promises about keeping secrets. I think you understand that, but I have to remind you anyway, officially. You know that we had your Assessment Review meeting today, and that I've written your report. But that's not necessarily the end of the story. If what you say now is relevant, I'll add it to the report. It'll be called an addendum, which just means a bit added on. Do you understand that?"

She doesn't give an answer, but she asks me, "Mr Warren, can I really trust you?" and I say, "In what way?" and she says, "Absolutely, can I trust you absolutely?", so I say, "I don't know. Let me think about that for a minute," and she says, "OK."

We both sit there in silence, and to me it feels powerful and important, but strangely, not uncomfortable. Maybe a minute goes by. Because of what's happened today, well, yesterday now, my thoughts keep returning to, and focusing on Dr M.

And maybe because of that, all of a sudden, I've got the words.

"Grace, let me tell you something, which I hope will answer your question. Years ago, in fact when I was just about the same age as you are now, I met someone who became very,

very important in my life. Someone who made all the difference to my life at that time. And this person said something which I've remembered ever since. She said, "The truth is like food for the mind. And lies are like poison." I believed in that when I first heard it, and I've believed in it ever since. So, when you ask if you can trust me, I can answer you with a promise, which is, I promise that, whatever you tell me, I'll be as truthful as I possibly can about it. I'll write it down as honestly as I can, and I'll tell you what I've written. I won't try to leave anything out, or to add to it, or to change it into something different."

After a short pause, Grace says, "OK. In that case, I'll tell you what happened when I shot my stepdad."

And I say, "OK. That's a deal."

Up until this moment, Grace had been an almost classic "No comment." Not absolutely silent when asked, during earlier police interviews, or by me as her report writer, or by various consultants, but she would say things like, "I don't want to talk about my stepdad, and I can't remember anything about what happened on the night he died." That was pretty much her standard line, and, with very slight variations, that was what she stuck to. But, for whatever quirks and twists of fate, time, mood and chemical cocktails in her brain, she was now ready to talk. And over the next two hours, talk she did.

She started off by saying, "I didn't always hate him, my stepdad. When he first met my Mum, a couple of years after my real Dad had buggered off, he seemed quite nice. He was generous, to me and my big brother, Jethro. He used to bring us

144

little presents, and give us money for sweets and ice-creams and stuff. But more than that, when he was around, my Mum used to be in a better mood, not so miserable and angry-looking as usual. And it wasn't as if we ever had a word from our real Dad, so really, this one felt like a better deal all round. When my stepdad wasn't there at home, Mum used to keep me and Jethro indoors all the time. Wouldn't let us out to play with our friends. Wouldn't let friends visit, either. But when he was there, I think Mum was just glad to see the back of us. So, thanks to him, we got more freedom plus occasional bribes. Not a bad deal."

At that point, Grace paused and looked as if she'd come to a grinding and painful stop. Exactly on cue, Louise came in with two cups of tea, saying, "Thought you might fancy a cuppa." As ever on the ball, Lou. Grace took a couple of sips. Me too. Then, without any prompt from me, she started up again.

"Of course, it all began to change as soon as he'd moved in. Almost straight away, he started acting like it was his house, and that he makes all the rules, for me, and Jethro, and for my Mum too. That's what they usually argued about. With Mum saying, 'It's my house, so what I say goes,' and him saying, 'As long as it's me paying the bills, and putting food on the table, you'll do what I fucking well tell you. All of you.'

"Meal-times were the worst. They turned into a nightly torture routine. We all had to sit down to eat dinner together, otherwise we wouldn't get any. And he'd sit there, thinking he's king of the castle, lording it over us all and whatever he says, it's like the bloody law. And he'd drink, one bottle of Guinness after another whilst he was eating, then whisky afterwards."

Grace took another long pause. Her voice was shaky, her whole body stiff.

I just waited, trying not to mirror her tension.

Eventually, she started speaking again:

"Anyway, on the night it happened, by the time he'd finished eating, he was already pissed. It was liver for dinner. I can't stand liver, and he knows that. And he told me, 'You aren't going anywhere till you finish what's on your plate'. And I can remember, pretty clearly, thinking to myself, 'I can't take this anymore. I can't stand being scared to death all the time, so I'm going to give the miserable bastard something to remember.

The shotgun had always been there, up on the wall above the fireplace. My real Dad had put it there. And he wanted everyone in the whole area to know it. He used to say. 'We're stuck halfway up the mountain, miles from our nearest neighbours, so, if anyone thinks of making an uninvited visit they should know we've got the gun, and it's loaded, and we all know how to use it,' all of which was true.

So, I'm sitting there, staring at the cold, half-eaten liver on my plate. Jethro's finished his, and he's been allowed to leave the table and go to his room. My stepdad says to my Mum, 'Clear the rest of the plates, and bring me my whisky glass.' then he turns his nasty drunk eyes on me. 'You, madam, make your mind up whether it's going to be your dinner tonight or your breakfast in the morning, whilst I fetch the scotch.'

Once Mum's on her way to the kitchen with her hands full of plates, and while he's getting his whisky out of the locked cupboard in the front room, I walk over to the mantle-piece, take down the shotgun, and go back to stand behind the dining-table. And I do know, exactly, what I'm thinking. I'm thinking that I'm going to point the gun straight at the bastard, give him the fright of his miserable fucking life, then blast both barrels straight into the ceiling, and then run for it.

"He walks back in, a full bottle of Bells in one hand, and a half-empty one in the other. He sees me with the gun, pointed straight at him, but instead of looking scared, he just gives me this sickening smile, and says, 'Well now, missy. And what do you intend to do with that gun?' So I tell him, 'Blow your bastard head off, both barrels.' That's what I said, and then my Mum is standing right next to me, and just as I'm on the point of raising the aim to the ceiling, and pulling the two triggers, she grabs the gun, half-way down the barrel and holds its aim. Dead steady, straight at his head, at the precise moment I shot. That's what happened. That's the truth. I feel glad he's dead, but I wasn't actually aiming to kill him."

And I say softly, "Jesus. Holy Jesus."

After a couple of breaths, I add, "OK. I'll write down what you've told me, word for word, as best I can. Then we'll look at it together, and you'll tell me if there's anything you want to change, or to add. OK?" and she says, "Yes, OK."

This is followed by a long, long silence. I have the feeling that she hasn't entirely finished, but I don't want to prompt or hurry or influence her in any way. So, we simply sit there. Eventually, she looks up at me, as if she's just come back from a whole world of inescapable isolation. Her voice is barely a whisper, but it seems to have found new depths of resolve. She says, "It wasn't true, what

I said before, that I couldn't remember what had happened. The truth is it's been the exact opposite. That I couldn't forget. Not a single bit of it."

And I say, "What you've said sounds and feels like the truth to me. And that's what I'll write, and it's what I'll say. Well done, Grace." There's another long pause, but this one feels comfortable and filled with relief.

I break it by asking, "How do you feel now?"

She gives one of those long, shuddering sighs, like little kids do when they've been bawling for ages, and then allow their mums to hold and soothe them. After a couple of normal, shallow breaths, she does another, slightly softer shudder. There is a gradual diminuendo, backed by the last receding waves of the aftershock.

At last she says, "Now, I feel just plain tired. And I feel as if it's safe now for me to go to sleep – for the first time since it happened."

I give her a brief hug, say goodnight, tell Lou that we're all done for now, that I'll tell her everything in the morning. Then I leave the unit, and fill my lungs with cool night air.

By the time I got outside, it was nearly half past three. Despite the fact that I'd been engrossed in and amazed by everything that had happened in the past couple of hours – that Grace had abandoned her no-comment position, the content of everything she'd disclosed – despite all that, within a couple of steps from leaving the unit, my mind was emptied of everything, apart from a vividly imagined picture of Dr M with Little Flo.

It was a still picture, no movement or action or dialogue.

Just the pair of them in this softly glowing peace and quiet. Dr M is sitting in her classic mode of, "I'm here, ready for anything you might say." Her feet are resting flat on the floor, weight evenly distributed, legs uncrossed. Her back's straight. Hands palms up, left gently clasped, thumbs just touching, resting relaxed in her lap. She's looking in Flo's general direction, but not straight at her.

And Flo is sitting there in a warm puddle of comfort, considering her choices of what to say, or to do next.

She has become un–dumbstruck.

That's the picture in my mind.

But in reality, as I walk up the path to our house, I see the light's on in our bedroom – a little yellow beam poking out through the gap in the curtains. I'm surprised, plus worried, in more-or-less equal measure. The flashback to my point of departure, the "Go then" from Fizz, weighs the scale comprehensively to the worried side.

There's a powerful waft of ganja as I walk up the stairs, and then I'm greeted by a billowing blue-black cloud of smoke as I open the bedroom door. Fizz is lying there, propped up by all the available pillows, ashtray planted in a fold of duvet over her belly. She gives me a big, dopey grin. "Hi, I'm glad you're back, Jack. Here, take this smoke bomb away from me. I seem to have rolled up more than I can manage. Eyes too big for my head."

I tell her I'm more than happy to relieve her of this problem, and I say I'm sorry for having been mean and snappy when I left earlier, and she says, "No, I'm sorry, Jack. That one was my fault. But anyway, I'm glad it happened 'cos it made me think. I couldn't sleep, and I wanted to talk to you, to say sorry and to say that I do understand about what your job's like. So, I rolled a solo joint, and pretended you were here with me, and had the conversation with you, without you. I answered for you too, and you've already accepted my apology and forgiven me, so you don't have to do it again now. Anyway, as soon as I'd sorted that one, I immediately started thinking…" And before she could say it, I did, and she did, so we chanted in unison, "About Dr M and Little Flo." Then we did a long "A'right" together.

After that, we talked, for maybe another hour. About all of the could-you-believe-it's that had conspired to land Dr M on our doorstep, to have her announce that she's involved in a research project, the subject of which is the effect of traumas on kids, about the traumatic facts and features of our own kid, and me saying for years that I wouldn't let any mad White-Coat psychos within a barge-pole's distance of Little Flo, because none of them would have been The One, and then The One appears, straight out of the clear blue sky. And we go through a bucket full of the predictable clichés of can't-believes and amazing coincidences and sometimes these things are just meant to happen, and the twists of fate and the turns of destiny, and the inscrutable meanings of life. That stuff.

By the time we've talked ourselves to a standstill, it's ten to five. I say, "I think I'm ready for sleep now." And Fizz says, "I'm not. Not yet. There's other stuff we need to do now." And with that, she puts the ashtray on the bedside cabinet, and pulls back the duvet, revealing the fact that she's seriously naked. And she says, "I haven't told you the whole of it yet. So while you weren't here, once I'd apologised to you, and, on your behalf, graciously accepted the apology, then I made you a promise, that at the very first opportunity, I would make it up to you.

So, get your clothes off, and get that great hulking body into bed with me, and lie back and think of England."

It would have been rude to refuse.

That was the night we made Little Flo's younger sister.

22

After mulling it over in my mind for a couple of days, I decided to have a cards-on-the-table chat with Dr Aveyleigh. For some while, my opinion of him, and previous prejudices against him, had been shifting. His starting position in my mind, from my initial job interview – all that bollocks about pronouncing De T, which, as far as I'm concerned, is entirely optional – anyway, to me at that time he had been a clever dick white coated smart, smug shithead. But the shift had started after he'd given me the connotative-versus-denotative number, which I could only acknowledge with a begrudging heart, whilst I also cherished a wish to discover a really good riposte of "Ah, yes, BUT!" with which I could confound him. But really, no buts.

Undoubtedly, he's a clever man, and on further acquaintance, his prickly shell and tendency towards two-upmanshippery reveals that it's his defensive strategy to protect an essentially good-natured heart. I'm not saying that I'd become totally smitten. Just that he'd migrated from being a pure white coat, to, I don't know what, maybe an off-white waistcoat, with some interesting bits of embroidery and a couple of intriguing bulges in the pockets.

The point is that I wanted to show my hand and declare my intent on the Dr M front. I rung his secretary, and said I'd like to see him about something which was a bit of a mixture of the personal and professional. I asked for a fifteen-minute slot. She said, "You may well be in luck, Jack. He was supposed to be seeing the Assistant Director at eleven this morning, but he's just phoned to cancel. I'll ask and call you back in a minute."

And, a minute later, she did, and said yes, and ten minutes later, I was in there.

A friendly greeting. "Good morning Jack. I'm pleased to see you. How can I help?" I apologised for the no-notice, thanked him for meeting me, and jumped straight in. "Dr Aveyleigh, you may remember from my application form, and from some of the discussion at my interview, that when I was a teenager, I spent a while in an adolescent psychiatric unit." He told me, yes, he remembered it well. So, without further ado, I told him that I'd met Dr Mandrake there, that I'd been her patient, and that she had completed my psychiatric Assessment Report as required by the court.

Now, either Dr Aveyleigh is a consummate actor, capable of an Oscar-winning pretence of shock, or this came as a pure out-of-the-blue bolt of really surprising news. He said, "Thank you for sharing this privileged information with me Jack, but you need not have done so. I am quite sure that Dr Mandrake would never do anything to breach client confidentiality." And I tell him I'm sure about that too, but I have a different reason for wanting him to know. Then I tell him about Little Flo, how she is now, how she used to be, what happened to Nancy. And I add that Dr Mandrake has mentioned her research project on kids and traumas. I say that I want to discuss with Dr M the possibility of her considering working with Little Flo, but that the fact of me being a former patient, with a daughter who's a prospective patient, and me also being a probable work colleague with Dr M at Beecliffe – well, that the whole thing feels complicated, and makes me want to spill beans now, rather than having future beans inadvertently escape if the lid were to come off the can.

Dr Aveyleigh says he sees my point. He says he wants a moment to reflect. I tell him he's welcome.

We share the moment quietly. Then he says, "Jack, I appreciate all that you have told me, and your motivation for having done so. Decisions about possible treatment for your daughter with Dr Mandrake are clearly hers, alone, to make. But I see no conflict of interest for her to do so. Furthermore, treatment for your daughter may entail, or may lead to work with either or both of her parents. Again, were this to transpire, I see no reason for your employment here to preclude or inhibit such work. I wish to assure you that this entire conversation is one which I shall hold in absolute confidence. And I would strongly recommend that you do likewise, and refrain from discussing any of these matters with colleagues – here or elsewhere."

I say that he has helped me clarify the situation in my own mind, and that I am truly grateful. And it's true.

This time, and really, for the first time, there are no clenched teeth at all.

So, with a rather jumbled mixture of feelings which include anxiety, excitement and hope, topped with an enormous sense of "thank God, at last," I decided I would write to Dr M.

Dear Dr M,

I've just finished a conversation with Dr Aveyleigh, in which you featured as the central topic. He was kind enough to give me your work address, and knows my purpose in writing to you.

As you no doubt recognised, it came as a huge surprise, and a literally shocking one, to see you at last week's review meeting. I felt as if I'd been scooped up by some demented time machine, and plunged back into my past, to re-live my tongue-tied traumas, the ones you saw when we first met. Fortunately, I was able to remember that I am now a grown-up, with a job, so that flashback to adolescence was a brief re-visit rather than a more sustained return. But, as I'm sure you can imagine, since the moment of our weird reunion last week my memory has been flooded with scenes and sensations of my time in the adolescent psychiatric unit.

I now feel that I'm over the initial surge of shock, and I'm left with a sense of delight that our acquaintance is renewed. I'm also full of hope that you may be able to help my daughter now as you helped me back then. Let me explain.

Little Flo, whom you met with me in the car park, suffered from a major trauma during her infancy. She was born one of two identical twins. Her sister was called Nancy. Both of them had a problem-free gestation, a relatively easy birth, and a perfectly happy infancy and early childhood together. Neither had any unusual or serious childhood illnesses, nor did they suffer injuries beyond the usual knocks, bumps and bruises of growing up. They were both normal, and in fact delightful kids. Then, when they were 15 months old, Nancy died. Initially, there was no obvious cause, but from the following post-mortem, the coroner's verdict was that of cot death. Nancy died at home during the night. I discovered her. Flo was in the same room with her. When I went in and found Nancy, Flo was standing up at the bars of her cot, adjacent to her sister's. She seemed to be in a state of petrified stillness and silence. And ever since that day, both Fizz, my wife, and I feel that we have lost the Flo we used to have – a vivacious, fun-loving, mischievous, spontaneous toddler. That Flo has gone, and she's been replaced by a child who constantly appears edgy and anxious, who hardly utters a word, who only acts, or interacts rarely, and when she does so, quickly retreats back into her tightly locked shell.

For years now, Fizz has been asking – in fact pleading with me to seek some support from the medical profession.

I have always adamantly refused. I have felt terrified that Flo would suffer at the hands of doctors, counsellors or psychiatrists – a terror which I realise is based in my own experiences. I hated, and reacted badly to, virtually every professional with whom I had contact as a teenager: apart, that is, from you. I do not say this to flatter, but as a simple statement of truth.

So, when you told me that you are now involved in a research programme into the effects of trauma on children, I felt as if I was being offered at least an opportunity, and possibly a genuine blessing.

Is it possible you could help us?
Please, let me know your thoughts.

With best wishes,
Jack Warren.

When I'd written the letter, I showed it to Fizz. She read it carefully, and said she thought it was fine, in fact she said she thought it was just perfect, so we sealed and stamped it, and both gave the envelope a little kiss, and wished it luck. Marley asked to join me on the half-mile walk to the local post box, whilst Flo stayed at home with Fizz.

Fizz and I made a pact. We promised to give it three days, during which we would not say a word about it.

Day three was up on Thursday. I was on a late shift plus sleep-in on Thursday night – but sleeping-in to my day off on Friday. I got home at quarter past eight, and in fact walked up our path with the postman.

"Morning Jack, just the one for you today." He gave me the letter, with its handwritten name and address. I recognised the writing. The postmark was from Newcastle.

As I'm going in through the front door, I'm simultaneously greeted by Marley, doing her happy crying twirling-round-in-circles tail-wagging routine, and also by Fizz. She's whispering, "Little Flo's had an awful night. Feverish. Sick twice. Nightmares, I think. Poor thing couldn't have slept for more than an hour. She seems a bit better now, and she's asleep so you better keep quiet, or I'll have to silently throttle you".

And I say, "OK, let's go in the dining room and have a cuppa while we read what Dr M's got to say."

Fizz says, "Please Jesus, make her be on our side."

The envelope's hand-written and so is the 'Dear Jack', but the rest is typed. I can't help myself. I do frantic scanning, and find "interested" followed by "need to obtain much more detail…" and then the Eureka of "will be pleased to undertake diagnostic…" And the whoopee of "hope and believe we shall be able to help." Once we've got the gist, we go back, and read it through, carefully, every word. She says that she had been extremely pleased to see the enthusiasm I showed for my work, and my skill in writing and delivering a complex Assessment Report. She says Dr Aveyleigh has spoken highly of me. She says how sorry she was to hear of Nancy's death, and that she recognised the pain this must have caused to all three of us. She says that she 'can easily imagine' the particular echoes and reverberations Nancy's death would have evoked in me, and adds something about death being universal, and at the same time unique to every individual in each instance.

She says that what I have described about Flo's reactions to Nancy's death strikes her as being extreme, but certainly not incomprehensible, and that she sees no reason to believe that at least an improvement, if not a full recovery should be possible for Flo. She says she wants to keep an open mind, but generally her expectation is that she would wish to undertake the work with me and Flo together, and subsequently, perhaps with all three of us. And she says she'd like to start, for a fifty-minute session, next Tuesday afternoon at three. She ends by suggesting that we tell Flo that her Daddy will be going to see a Doctor with her, and that Daddy used to know this Doctor when he was young, and felt that he'd been helped by her when he was struggling with some difficult problems in his life. And, finally, she says, if we feel unsure about how to answer any questions from Flo, not to think too long and hard about it, but to trust our instincts.

We say, "Wow." And, "Right then." And, "Next Tuesday." And "Mmm."

23

It's Tuesday lunchtime. I've had to do a bit of juggling to get the afternoon off, and I've called in two specific favours, but now the rota is sorted out, and Fizz, Flo and I are finishing our treacle puddings and custard, before Flo and I set off to see Dr M in Newcastle. Fizz says, "Flo, do you understand where you and Daddy are going this afternoon, and what it's for?"

Flo replies with a complete, and I think, rather elegant answer. "To see that lady who smells like Grandma, and find out if I'm sad."

Fizz says, "Aah, I see. Do you want to go?" And Flo says,

"Yes, 'cos I like to go in the car. And it smells nice too. But not like Grandma."

This conversation, in which Flo is a genuine participant, stands as a reasonable example of where we've got to now. It's been fairly rapid, and sustained progress since her landmark of, "Sorry Nanny, I didn't mean to."

When we're at home, and it's just the three of us, and as long as we're all reasonably relaxed and stress-free, we quite often have these exchanges in which Flo will say something – always in response to a question, or some other type of prompt – and sometimes she'll also allow a brief afterthought to slip out. But, so far at least, she never initiates talk, and she definitely doesn't do chatting. And never wonders out loud. If she has an available answer to a question, there's a fair chance she'll say it, but she never says, "Don't know," or, "Not sure," let alone, "I wonder if…"

But, in comparison to the almost constantly silent Flo of just a few months ago, progress has been amazing. And that's the thought in my head whilst we're driving up the A1. Flo's in the back seat, on a cushion, safely belted, Ted clasped to her neck, looking out of the window. The car's still pretty new, which is why Flo and I think it smells nice, but certainly nothing like Grandma.

We're listening to J.J. Cale on the car cassette. And I'm thinking to myself, if Flo's making all this progress without any assistance, maybe we should just let her be. Why risk upsetting her apple-cart? What kind of pain and grief and God-knows-what-else is Dr M going to stir up for the poor kid? Why don't

I just get off the motorway at the next exit, turn round and head back down south?

What a thought. And how superficially attractive it seems. So, why not?

Well, I suppose the serious chance that Fizz would kill me, that's one answer to why not. That prospect should be considered, weighed carefully, respected.

We keep going north. Then all of a sudden, my head is back on that train from Leeds to Darlington on my way to the Beecliffe interview, thinking I can't bear the prospect of having to leave Otley; thinking, actually, I don't have to. I can choose. And once the choice is realised, I'm able to make it and take it, accept the challenge.

The sign says, "Services, 1 mile", so I decide, right, I'll pull up in the car park, which I do. Turn off the engine. Get in the back seat with Flo. Hold her little face in my oversized mitts. Say to her, "Flo, are you nervous or worried about seeing Dr M?" And without pausing for breath or to blink, she says "No Daddy, you are!" She's right, spot on. I say, "Shall we go then, to see Dr M?" Flo nods, no wavering.

We arrive at the hospital. Ask at reception. Get directions to go along miles of corridors. Shiny lino. That smell. White coats everywhere. Flo holds my hand. We arrive at the door. Read the nameplate. Dr Carol Mandrake. Senior Consultant Psychiatrist. Lots of letters after her name. We knock and wait. Almost immediately, she's standing there. Warm smile. "Hello Jack, and hello Flo, do come in."

We walk into her office. I see it, and I can't believe it.

The desk is different. The room is different. But, in the corner, there are those four, low, comfy chairs, the even lower coffee table, and the plant, with pink hairy stems. I look at it all, and say, "Well, good heavens," and Dr M says, "So much in life is always changing. I like it when I can keep some things the same."

We all sit down. Dr M in her chair, me in mine, but this time the one between us in the middle isn't empty. Flo takes it, clasping Ted to the side of her neck. Dr M says, "Flo, do you know why your Daddy brought you here to see me?"

Silence.

Dr M allows a little pause, but before it starts to feel too uncomfortable, she says, "It's OK, Flo. I'm not going to keep asking you loads of questions at the moment, but, anytime you want to ask me anything, or you want to say something, just go ahead." Flo nods her head, twice. And because Ted is cradled in her neck, this movement makes him nod too, which makes all three of us smile – Dr M and I to each other, Flo to her freshly polished Clark's sandals.

Dr M is still smiling, and still looking directly at me, and says, "OK, then. Jack, would you like to say why you have brought Flo to see me today?" And I say, "Yes, I would, although it might come out a bit jumbled." Dr M says that jumbled is just fine, and that jumbled is quite normal, and in fact, jumbled is what you get when you first tip out all the pieces from the box, when you're going to make a jigsaw puzzle, but that you have to tip the pieces out of the box in order to see which ones fit together, so you can start to make the picture. Flo says, "I like jigsaws." Dr M says,

"Good, will you help with this one?" And Flo and Ted nod in unison. Dr M smiles, bigger this time, revealing that gold tooth, the one next to the left incisor.

I begin. Pieces tumble from the box, and I pick them out, turning them the right way up. There's the piece which shows the first time I met Dr M and felt comfortable with her, straight away. There's another piece, which shows my face, with a big clamp over my lips, stopping me from talking. Another piece shows the inside of a church, with a coffin. And right next to it, a different church, this time with a tiny little coffin. And there are two pieces I pick up together. One of them is baby Flo, full of life and mischief. The other is Flo at her birthday party, with my best friend Charley, but this Flo seems to be frozen stiff, full of fear and misery. There's a piece which shows me grasping the edges of an enormous sticking plaster which covers half my chest and all of my belly, and it's stained, dark browny-red with patches of sickly yellow. And there's a final one, of Flo, looking a couple of years older than she is now – looking like she's come back to life.

All those jigsaw pieces come out quickly from the jumbled pile. I just pick them up one at a time, say briefly what they look like, place them face up on the table, and move on to the next. The whole thing takes no more than three or four minutes. Flo and Dr M watch me, and listen, without saying a word. I tell them I've stopped. Dr M says, "I think we've already got lots of interesting pieces, and I'm sure it's going to take us a few goes before we can complete the picture, to see what the whole thing looks like." She then turns to Flo. "Will you join in, and help us to complete the jigsaw picture, because I think that not all the

164

pieces can come just from your Daddy. Some of them belong to you, and we'll need them to finish the picture properly."

Flo says, "I will help with the jigsaw puzzle. That's easy. But, really, I just think Daddy's too unhappy. Can you make him better?"

Dr M says, "I'll certainly try my best."

Dr M then looks directly at Flo, and she says, "What do you think about these pieces of the jigsaw that your Daddy has just shown us?"

Flo says, "I think that the picture of the little coffin is Nancy. She's my sister. She died when we were babies."

Dr M tells Flo she thinks she's right. And that she thinks Flo will be a great help, finding the pieces which fit together.

Then she continues. "We've got a big job to do. It's not going to be quick or easy to find all the pieces we need. But that's OK. Your Mummy may be able to help us too because she'll have some more of the pieces. Your Daddy has already told me that Mummy wants to help us with the puzzle.

"Anyway, at the moment, I don't know what the finished picture will look like. None of us can really see it, yet. And I do expect that, when we look at some of the pieces by themselves, they're going to seem hard to recognise, and some of them might feel quite scary. But, as long as we can be brave, and look at them, even the scary ones, it will help us to put the picture together, and when we can look at the whole picture, the scariness will not be nearly as scary anymore. I feel really sure, that one of the things which will help us on this puzzle, is the fact that your Daddy and I have already worked on a different one, years ago. And some of the pieces we used to make that picture are the same as, or nearly the same as the ones we're working with now. That will make the job a bit easier. And I think that's why your Daddy asked me to help again this time. What do you think, Flo?"

Flo says, "I get scared, 'specially when Daddy's unhappy, 'cos I think he's going to be angry."

I don't say it out loud, but I see it, crystal clear. There's me, with that great big sticking plaster, which is starting to give out a nasty smell. And right next to me, there's Little Flo. Not a sticking plaster for her. No, she's swaddled from head to toe, in yard after yard of bandage, wrapped tight, round and round. She's mummified. She can hardly move at all. There's a tiny hole at the mouth which is just big enough to breathe through, and, occasionally, let an odd word slip out. But for the moment, I keep all that to myself.

Dr M tells us that it's nearly time to finish for today. She asks Flo if she'd like to come back next week, when we can work some more on our jigsaw. Flo and Ted nod. Dr M says she's glad, but before we go, she wants to show something to Flo.

Behind her desk, there's a great big cupboard. Floor to ceiling, with double wooden doors. She opens it. On one side, there are drawers, all locked shut, each one with a name stuck to the front. On the other side, bigger, deeper drawers. She pulls one open. It's full of model animals – farmyard sheep and pigs and cows, big scary-looking monsters, cute furry chimps and teddy bears, plus a couple of snakes. In another drawer, there are all sorts and sizes of dolls, and lots of costumes and outfits to dress them up in. The final drawer she opens has paper, crayons, paints, plasticine. A treasure trove of toys. Flo looks, amazed. Dr M says, "Next time you come, you can play with anything you choose. And look, there's one drawer which is especially for you. I've written your name on it already."

Sure enough, there she is, Little Flo, second from the top. "So, if you do any pictures or drawings, or if you make any models from plasticine, we'll keep it all safe, locked away, just for you." Flo says, "We'll like that." And Dr M says, "Good, see you next week." And she shakes hands, first with Flo, then me.

On the way back home in the car, Flo seems quiet, but peaceful. I ask her if she liked Dr M. She says "Mmm." I ask if she's looking forward to coming back next week. "Mmm," again. I ask if she wants to hear the other side of J.J. Cale, or something different, and she tells me to choose, so it's more J.J.

I concentrate on the driving, but immediately get absorbed by, and lost in my own thoughts.

But, for the next few miles, every time I check in the rear-view mirror, I can see Flo, and Ted.

Something's different. Ted isn't in his usual position, with his face buried in Flo's neck, just below her ear. No, now she's holding him with both hands in front of her. They're having an animated, but really soft and warm, conversation. Face to face. She keeps telling him stuff. He listens and nods. A couple of times, I get a glimpse of Ted whispering in Flo's ear. Occasionally, Flo shakes her head in obvious disagreement. But mostly, she's nodding with enthusiasm. And amazingly, she smiles so fully that I can see her teeth.

Now, the last time I can remember seeing those teeth in a smile, they were brand new, and milky white and she only had a few of them. That set me thinking.

When we got home, Flo ran up the drive to meet her Mummy who was standing there at the open door. Flo said, "Ted really likes Dr M. He wants to see her again next week. She's got great big boxes full of toys and dolls. We're going to play with them. Daddy's coming too."

And Fizz says, "That's just wonderful. I'm so pleased for you. So, when can I come?"

Flo says, "Soon."

24

Teeth.

Seeing Flo's in the rear-view mirror, smiling at Ted – well more like gleeful grinning at times – it came as a shock. Not so much the shock of seeing them, as the shock of realising how used we were to not seeing them. How literally tight-lipped Flo had become.

Anyway, teeth got me thinking.

I'm taking Marley for a late-night walk. She's obviously grateful, having spent most of the day cooped up in the house. We're in the woods, under a clear sky and a nearly full moon. I'm keeping to the path, which is easy to see. She keeps dashing off into dense dark woods. I whistle her to heel, and with a sudden crackling and breaking of bracken, she appears – jet-black dog from jet-blacker undergrowth. I say to her, "Come on Marls, over here. Give us a smile." She wags her tail, pushes against my thigh with her head, jumps up with front paws on my belly, half a yard of pink tongue lolling out. For her, she's surely smiling. I say, "Get down Marley," and as she does, I go down on my knees, lowering myself, bringing our heads level. I'm stroking the back of her head with one hand, and then take her snout in the other. With my thumb, I raise a bit of her lip, and expose her upper canine. She growls. I cover the canine. She stops. Expose it again, she growls again. It seems to me as if the physical act of exposing that tooth gets an automatic growl response. Nothing to do with the mood she's in, before, or after. Interesting.

All of which gets me thinking about Flo's teeth, and the baring of them, or not. So far, she's only showing them to Ted, and then only when she seems to be feeling warm and friendly, and comfortable. But does she know that teeth can signal a warning, can say, "Keep your distance"? Can be used as weapons to hurt and harm?

And I'm not at all sure, how or why, but all this tooth-thinking brings back to mind the image, from this afternoon's session with Dr M, of Flo, swaddled, bound from head to toe, wrapped-and-strapped up, foot to mouth. Like a picture of the invisible man. With just that tiny hole in the middle of the face mask. Barely enough to breathe through, and seemingly small and constricting enough to ensure that hardly a word can escape. How did she get so mummified? How could she manage to insulate and isolate herself so completely? I could just about imagine why. I'm guessing it's to protect herself from the dangerous world outside those layers of bandage. I can guess why, but how? It's hard enough to bandage your own finger, or hand. But your whole body? Obviously impossible.

Then I see it, all of a sudden, all in one go. A ghastly revelation. Oh, holy shit.

It's suddenly obvious. It's me. It's what I've done to her. I've moved on from my own self-applied, self-adhesive great big plaster, to wrapping Flo into a cocoon that's just about succeeded in turning her lights out. I've not been saving her. More like strangling her, with yards of sterile bandage. Oh, Jesus.

Maybe, to avoid being totally suffocated, she's used her teeth. She's managed to bite through the bandages from the inside. She's bitten out a hole, just big enough to breathe through, to keep herself alive. But there's no space, or chance to grow.

An awful case of arrested development.

A fatal trap, in a crippling cocoon.

25

Fizz

Now, I'm well and truly muddled.

Once Jack and Flo had set off to see Dr M, I sank into a kind of nervy daydream. I couldn't settle to anything, just mooched around the house. It seemed like I'd infected Marley, who also did a spell of wandering and whining. I decided to take her for a walk, but turned round and came home after five minutes. Then we sat on the sofa together, fretting. Watching the clock, which seemed to have decided on a go slow.

Eventually, I fell into an anxious doze, from which I woke up with a start when Marley jumped down from the sofa, announcing that they'd be home in another couple of minutes. As usual, she was right. The shiny little Escort estate pulled round the corner, parked, and a few seconds later, Flo is running up the path to our front door, looking…different. Not sure what at first, till I realised it was excited.

Fantastic.

Before I had a chance to ask or say anything, Flo was telling me she'd liked meeting Dr M, and what's more, was looking forward to seeing her again. It was all better than I'd dared to dream.

Jack too, he seemed to be relaxed, maybe relieved. But there was a shadow hanging over him. His mind was obviously chewing on some big bone, and his body looked and felt tense.

We had tea together, which was OK. Flo was almost falling asleep at the table, so I told her, "Right, bath, short story and early to bed for you." She gave a "No arguments from me" nod, so we finished up, left Jack to clear and wash the dishes, had the bath and bubbles, and by half past six, she was in bed.

A couple of months beforehand, I'd read *The Wind in the Willows* to her. It took a week or two, and she seemed to just soak up the story like a dried-out pot plant getting watered at last. She asked for it again tonight as she and Ted were getting into bed. She said, "Not the beginning. Just the part where Mole smells his old home, and he has to go in."

I find the right bit, and read the stuff about Mole, how he'd abandoned his home on that bright spring morning, and hadn't really thought of it since, then realised how much he'd been missing it. And even though it was cold and dark and empty

173

when he and Ratty went in, it was still home. So they lit a fire, and found a meagre supper, but were then visited by the carol-singing mice, and one was sent out to bring back all sorts of goodies, and then they ate till they were all full up, and everyone was warm and tired and happy. And once we got to that bit, Flo said, "That's it. Stop there, no more now!"

I closed the book and put it down. As I was bending down to kiss Flo goodnight, she held me, and gave me a fierce hug. She whispered in my ear. "Daddy's still too sad. But I'm sure we'll make him better now."

And I say, "What about you, Flo? Are you too sad?" and she says, "A bit too sad. But not so scared now." As I'm walking downstairs, thinking, "Thank you Jesus, for being on our side," I see that Jack is taking his coat off the hook and inviting Marley to go walkies. As he's going out of the door, he's got that worried face on. He just about manages to mumble something about having to sort his head out.

When he comes back an hour and a half later, he looks haunted and deranged.

26

It wasn't that late, maybe just gone half nine. I'd been out for about an hour and a half. I was tempted to stay out longer, to make sure that Fizz would already have gone to bed before I got back, but I was gagging for a joint and a drink. I didn't even have a roll-up with me – or any money – otherwise I'd have gone into the Duke of Cambridge, where Marley and I are regular and welcome guests.

Walking up our front path, it looked re-assuring at first. All dark downstairs, bedside lamplight peeping through the curtains from our room. Marley and I let ourselves in. I ease the front door shut. Marley does big noisy shaking. Fizz calls down, "You home? you OK?" I say, "Yes and no". Dumb mistake!

"No? No what?"

I say, "No, nothing, nothing really. Just stuff that got stirred and shaken up from this afternoon." My voice obviously lacks any calm conviction to back up the words I'm saying.

Fizz says, "Jack, I can hear you're not right. And I could see it on your face when you bolted out of here with Marley. You can't just keep bottling it up inside. It's poisonous. And not just for you. I'm coming down. We're going to talk."

What could I say? "No, I refuse"? Hardly. She's halfway down the stairs, wearing my dressing gown, tying the belt, rolling up the sleeves. She looks straight at me. What I feel is fear and dread. I think what she sees in my expression looks like anger, resentment and hostility. Mismatch. Misunderstandings leading to missiles being launched with implacable force. Oh dear, oh dear.

The whole fucking apple-cart, whoosh like Vesuvius.

"What are you so angry about?"

"I'm not angry!"

True at the start of the statement, false by the end.

"Don't think to yourself that you're going to frighten me into silence this time!"

"That's not fair!"

"You're damn right, it's not fair!"

Every barb snags on sore flesh, rips, hurts, ramps up the reply. Rivers of resentment, bottled-up, stored away, saved for such a special occasion – breach the damn – defences down, the torrent gushes over the flood plains.

It's rare for me and Fizz to have these red-in-tooth-and-claw fights. Maybe if we had them a bit more often, there'd be less backlog, fewer poison darts. I think that we both get frightened in these situations, and too scared to admit it, so we end up hiding the real fear beneath layers of diverting hostility – constantly missing the point, but slashing and burning in an orgy of bile-letting warfare.

Fizz fires off some familiar rounds about me thinking I'm so smart, and hiding behind barricades of clever words, but really not having as much understanding about feelings as a dumb ten-year-old. She fires off taunts of, "So, lost for words now, are you? You emotional dwarf. You fucking oaf."

And I want to say that I've just realised that it's been me, my fault. That I've been tying Little Flo up in a straitjacket, but the words just stick in my throat, as if I'm trying to swallow a handful of aspirins with no glass of water. So instead, I spit out a sarcastic mouthful of how sorry I am not to be as fucking perfect and tolerant and sweet-tempered as she is. To which I get the stunning reply,

"She was right, my mum, what she said about you. She said I should stay away from you – that you'd only bring me a heap of misery. She said I should avoid you like the plague. She called you the White Death."

This one comes out in one thick, sick stream. Stinking projectile vomit.

The moment Fizz says it, I see that Little Flo is standing there in the open doorway. She looks really serious, and absolutely determined. She says, in a small but clear voice, "You mustn't shout like that. You'll scare the baby."

I don't catch her meaning. I say to her, "I'm sorry Flo. Didn't mean to frighten you, or upset you," and she says, "No, not me. You have to not shout 'cos of the baby. You have to promise."

And I say, "OK sorry, Flo. I promise", but although my promise is heartfelt, I haven't understood, yet.

I take Flo back upstairs, and spend ten minutes soothing and settling her. I tell her that it can happen, that you can be angry and upset with someone, but it doesn't mean you've stopped loving them. She tells me it'll be OK and that she, with some help from Dr M, will stop me being too sad anymore. She's ready to sleep, so she rolls over, fishes Ted out from under her pillow, clasps him to her neck, and says, "Night, night."

As I walk downstairs, I hear the clinks and tinkles of Fizz making tea for two. Coming out of the kitchen, she says, "It was only half true, really. It was true that my mum said you were bad news – White Death, in fact. But it wasn't true, and it isn't true that I agree with her, or believe her!"

I tell her that I'm glad that I married her, and not her mum, and she says, "Me too."

The venom has gone. The boil's been lanced, and in fact now we have a rare opportunity to look a bit deeper, to snatch a glimpse at the roots which anchor and feed these rare but bitter flowers.

There is a pattern to our rows. We often teeter on the brink for a long while, and then there's the sudden explosion. Generally, it's Fizz who does most of the yelling, whilst I do nasty bits of re-evaluation, cleverly pointing out the weaknesses in her arguments, the inherent contradictions, the illogical connections, the emotional injustices. All of which maddens her further and goads her to greater excesses of accusations and allegations which I denounce, and denigrate, and vehemently deny. And generally, once we're done, I tend to mount a high-horse – assuming the role of a victim of gross calumnies, a martyr to injured pride. I sit on this noble charger, and sulk, silently and insufferably, sometimes for days.

But somehow, this time, Little Flo's intervention seems to have short-circuited the whole programme. Fizz says, "Let's have our tea, and talk properly." And I say, "Yes, let's. And what's she on about, 'You'll frighten the baby?'" Fizz says, "That's part of what we've got to talk about."

But still I haven't got a clue.

27

Fizz

Pregnant!

Actually, now I think it must be true. Before I thought it was some kind of metaphor – a symbol, where you had to think hard to work out the hidden meaning. But now, I think it is literally true. And I'm pretty sure that's what Flo thinks too, so no need to try and interpret or analyse her position on the fact, though its meaning to her, that's another story.

After we'd read that passage from *Wind in the Willows*, I'd thought that she'd dropped off to sleep more or less immediately. I was pottering around in the kitchen for the next half hour, then went upstairs to the loo, then just stood quietly at Flo's open bedroom door. Without any movement, a voice comes out of the apparently sleeping body. "Mummy, can you sit with me for a minute?" I say, "Sure I can". She shifts back to make some space for me, and I sit, half way down the bed, stroking the shining black hair spreading over her pillow. She's lying on her left side, and brings her right arm out from the duvet and holds my hand, which is resting in my lap. She's still and quiet for a moment, then her hand releases itself from mine, then hovers, then lands, soft as a feather, on my belly. Just below the button.

She says, "Is it Nancy, the baby? Do you think she'll come back now?" I tell her I don't know. We'll have to wait and see. I ask her, how does she know about the baby. She just says "I think it's Nancy. I think she wants to come back home now, so I think we should all look after her very carefully this time." I say that I think she's right about that, and after a short pause, she says, "I think that Dr M. knows that Daddy needs to get Nancy back so he won't be too sad any more, and me too, and you. So that's why I think Dr M's put the baby in your tummy."

I tell Flo that I think she's at least partly right because I believe that I do have a brand-new baby in my tummy, plus I tell her I think she's ever so right that we'll all have to try our best to take care of it.

But I can hardly believe it. Within an hour of saying all that to Flo, I'm yelling my head off at Jack, in an absolute rage. That look on his face, when he went out of the door with Marley, it was so full of "Help me, I'm lost," but by the time he got back, his whole body was clenched, and all I could manage was to pour every drop of petrol I could lay my hands on, pour it straight onto my burning anger, and hope to blow Jack's defences and silence to kingdom-fucking-come. And, if he dares to try on his sulking routine, I'm going to climb up on a chair, grab him by the throat, and throttle him till he pleads for forgiveness. That's what I decided whilst I was making the tea, and he was tucking Little Flo back in her bed.

Once we're settled on the sofa, Jack gets straight into his, "What's all this baby business?" questioning. So, I cut to the chase. I tell him I'm pregnant. He says "How's that possible?" I say, "Usual way!" he says, "How, exactly, when we haven't made love in months and months, apart from when you wantonly seduced me a couple of weeks ago, and…" before he expands this last "and…", I tell him, "Yes, exactly. Two weeks ago. And I just knew it, immediately and certainly. Then I thought maybe not. Maybe it was a wish-fulfilling fantasy, or some Freudian hysterical stuff. But now, I'm sure, for sure. I know we've made a baby. Strange thing is that Flo somehow knows it too. Stranger still, or maybe not, she thinks the baby is Nancy, coming home. Strangest of all, she thinks, that Dr M put the baby in my tummy. So what do you make of that little lot then?"

He says, "I just don't know, don't know what to make of it. But I do know, how I feel, about this baby. I've had the feeling before. It's called delighted."

And I say "Really? Me too."

We both take sips of tea. Marley pads across, lays her large black head in my lap, and asks nicely for me to tickle behind her ears and massage her neck and shoulders. I'm happy to oblige. While I'm looking at the pooch, I say to Jack, "When are you going to tell me what it is that's troubling and hurting you so badly?"

And he says, "Now. I'll tell you right now."

28

I launch, more or less straight into it.

"Fizz, you know about my great big imaginary sticking plaster?" She says, "Only sort of", so I give her more chapter and verse, and she gets the picture, why, and what for, back then; why it's back on the agenda now, perched in the front of my mind. I tell her the plaster has started to smell bad, and that it's beginning to curl up at the edges, and that, instead of just desperately trying to stick it back down, I feel like I want to look and see what it is that the plaster's covering – let in a bit of light and air.

She says "Mmm, sounds like pulling it off could be painful, especially if hairs are stuck to it."

I say "Mmm" too, then, "Not only hairs. Innards."

"Oh."

She sees.

Anyway, it's not about me and my plaster at the moment. That's what I tell her. She looks unconvinced. I say, "No. Honestly. It's about Flo. I saw it clearly for the first time this afternoon. It was like a complete vision. Little Flo, tightly bandaged, head to toe. And at first, I thought, she's just like her Dad. She's been hurt, so she's had to protect herself. And in doing so, she's reduced herself to a lifeless mummy. And I thought to myself, how clever I'd been to realise what she'd done and why.

"But something wasn't right. Something was untrue about this bandaged-up kid. And this evening, I realised what. You can't wrap yourself up as a mummy. It's clearly impossible. Someone else has to do it. And that someone, in this particular case, is me. I'm the one. It isn't that Flo was like me. It's that I've done it to her. All this time, I've prevented her from grieving for her sister, which has stopped her from growing – or from having anything like a life."

"OK, Jack. And how, exactly, do you think you've managed it?" This sounds like a reasonable question. No sarcasm or mocking in the tone. I tell Fizz that I don't know how, exactly, but refusing to allow anyone to help Flo, doctors or whoever – probably has been part of the problem. That, plus my embargo on any mention of Nancy's name – no photos, toys, visible reminders of any sort.

There's a bit of a natural pause, after which I say that now, it all feels like I've created a great conspiracy of denial. Denial of Nancy's very existence, and that I've wrapped Flo up as an enforced mute – co-opted into my regime of silence.

Fizz reckons that this could well be a part of the story, but insists that it's only a part, not the whole thing. She also says something which I think is both smart and helpful.

"If you've had a serious injury which requires you being bandaged up, think what has to happen when the dressing needs to be changed. Someone, who knows what they're doing, has to very carefully, bit by bit, start to remove the bandage, to see how the healing is progressing. They don't say 'enough of this' and rip the whole lot off in one go. It would hurt too much. And, obviously, it could cause some serious damage."

True, that's true.

29

On Thursday morning, there's a letter for me, all hand-written.
It says:

Dear Jack,

*I'm writing to you, individually, to put to you a suggestion
which I want you to consider. This is something connected
to the work we have now begun with Flo – and, at the same
time, it's something distinct and separate.*

I wish to offer you the opportunity to undertake some

individual work with me. Initially, I would envisage us having two sessions, the first of which would be focused on making sure that we have achieved reasonable endings for the work which we undertook when you were my patient at the Adolescent Unit. Hopefully, this will enable us to identify any loose ends, tie them off safely, and hence ensure that they're not going to obscure or confuse our present work. The second session would then shift the focus onto openings, in an attempt to "prepare the ground" for the ensuing work with Flo. This may seem odd, given that the three of us have already had our first session, but my intuition tells me that the proposed one-to-one work with you could be helpful. What's more, my supervisor strongly supports such an initiative. I have now had my first supervision session for my work with you and your family, and I will continue to receive this support on a weekly basis, for as long as our work continues. I am relieved that this is the case, and, in fact, would not have felt able to proceed were it not so. To the best of my knowledge, the situation in which we now find ourselves is unique, comprising as it does a client who is a past patient, a present work colleague, and an integral part of a family who wish to work together in order to address a specific trauma and its aftermath. We have a fascinating Venn diagram of separate, interlocking and overlapping elements, in which borders and boundaries will be of critical importance. We would ignore, or underestimate, this fact at our peril. Equally, in recognising this reality, we will have, I feel sure, a rare opportunity to promote healthy growth for all.

My research work into the effects of trauma on young people and their families is fully funded for the next three years. Consequently, although my invitation for you to accept individual psychotherapy sessions is both formal and "official", you would incur no financial cost.

Please let me know your thoughts on this matter as soon as you can. The joint work with you, your daughter, and subsequently your wife too, can proceed irrespective of your decision about working individually with me.

I look forward to hearing from you.

With best wishes,
Dr M

Well, well.

My immediate reaction was one of visceral red-hot rage.

There was me, thinking that poor Little Flo was the one with the trauma, even if I was the one who'd landed her with it. Thinking it was her problem, that she was the one who needed the treatment, or intervention, or psychotherapy – or whatever.

This is the picture in my head. I see Dr M coming back on the scene, as if by magic, and there she is, able to cure Flo, in the same way that she'd previously cured me.

Or not. Maybe she never really did cure me in the first place. Maybe I've remained a constant half-nut, who occasionally flares brightly as a full-blown lunatic. Maybe Dr M is not half as fucking clever as she thinks. Or as I used to think. Maybe she just sees Flo, and me, as an interesting feature of her well-funded research project – there to be exploited and used to her advantage. Perhaps Flo and I are mere cannon-fodder for an illuminating chapter in her ground-breaking book.

This must be the first time I've ever had such doubts in my mind about Dr M. Up till now, she's been the perfect, all-powerful, absolute source of salvation and redemption. The absolute, ultimate, ideal object.

Maybe I'm angry, because I've just allowed myself the thought that Dr M could be less than totally perfect.

Maybe I'm angry, but can't quite decide, or realise, who I'm angry with.

And, maybe like Flo, I've got teeth – which just could have the potential to be bared in anger, and to bite, with venom.

Smile, Jack. And maybe snarl a little.

I pick up a pen and notepad, and fire off a furious letter to Dr M. I accuse her of thinly veiled self-interest, of being a low-life quack, whose driving ambition is to secure her own fame and fortune, constructed on the wreckage of other's innocent misfortunes and tragic traumas. I absolutely reject the prospect of my daughter being offered as a further sacrifice to Dr M's naked and hollow ambitions. And, with a final flourish of excess, tell her that I hereby refuse to immolate myself beneath the wheels of her juggernaut of heartless hubris.

This last bit is, I recognise, so wildly over the top that it's laughable. And I do laugh, till the tears roll down, and the searing anger is gently transformed, at least in that moment into a heart which can ache with a pain which is, just, bearable.

I screw the letter into a tight ball, which I fling at the waste-paper basket. It bounces off the wall and, improbably, lands plumb centre. I raise my right fist, celebrating the three-pointer.

I take a fresh piece of paper, and write a short and simple letter – basically saying, "Thank you, Dr M, I'd love to."

Envelope, address, stamp, stick. Call the dog. Before leaving the room, I extricate the first draft from the basket, carefully unfold, and re-read it.

I get the feeling that I just might have some juicy material to work on.

30

I just managed to catch the last collection for the post on Thursday evening, sending off my short, sane acceptance of the offer from Dr M. Evidently, she received it the next morning, because at lunch time in my office, I had a call from reception, giving me the message to phone Dr M on the following number, "When you've got a few minutes to talk." Having a few minutes, let alone the reliable prospect for privacy, doesn't happen on the unit. I tell Alan, the shift leader, that I need to go home for half-an-hour, without explaining why. He says, "Fine, but don't forget your one o'clock pre-assessment meeting with the Ed Psych." With a quick,

"Will do. Thanks for reminding me," I'm off.

I get home to an empty house – no Fizz, Flo or Marley. This feels like a relief.

There's a knot in my stomach, my palms are sweating, and all of a sudden I've got a pounding head-ache. I have a brief flirtation with the thought of not calling, then put it aside, and shakily pick up the receiver. I get through to Dr M's secretary straight away, and she says that the doctor is expecting my call, but that she is in with a client at the moment, will be finished in fifteen minutes, and has asked if she could call me then. I say quite calmly, that's fine, and give my home number.

I hang up, and then feel a surge of fury. In my head I have a vicious voice saying, "What is the fucking point of telling me to ring her when I've got a minute, and then locking herself away with some other fucking client? Stupid, selfish bitch."

I look at my watch. 12.35. That means she'll ring twenty-odd minutes before my one o'clock. If she's prompt. Bollocks. Don't know what to do. Dithering flap. Don't know whether to laugh or cry. Try both, doesn't help. Toy with the idea of a quick secretive spliff. Feel tempted. Stand there, with my hand six inches from the stash box, hovering. The phone rings. I jump, literally. Both feet off the ground. On landing, I pat myself on the chest a few times, trying to encourage my heart to keep going, but maybe not quite so hard and fast. Pick up the receiver. Say a half–strangled "Hello."

It's my Ma, who asks, "You OK, Jack? You sound peculiar."

"Yes Ma, I'm fine, just expecting you to be someone else."

Ma says yes, her too, she was expecting me to be Fizz, and

what am I doing at home when I should be at work. I say I can't explain now, and I can't talk 'cos of the other call I'm waiting for. Ma says to give a message for Fizz to phone her back. I say will do, and that I'll call her when I've got more than a breathless moment – at the weekend. She says OK. I say, "Bye Ma", and hang up.

Within less than ten seconds of the receiver going down, the phone rings again. I jump, again. This time it is Dr M. She asks if I'm OK, says I sound tense. I tell her I'm anxious because I have to be back at work in a few minutes for a meeting.

She asks if I can come to her office tomorrow morning at 10.00. I tell her I can, she says, "Good, see you then."

I say, "Thanks, Ma," and hang up.

Walking back to the unit, I clock the fact that I've called Dr M, "Ma." I say to myself that this must be a piece of Freudian slippery. But the truth is, I don't have a clue.

Truth is, I do have a clue, loads of clues in fact, but I just don't get it.

31

Saturday morning. Five to ten. Fifty yards between me and Dr M's office. I do a bit of loitering. Don't want to be caught standing, obviously, outside her door. I walk down the corridor, in the opposite direction to Dr M's office. Another corridor intersects. Above it, a sign with arrows pointing to X-ray and Toilets. Great, just time for a quick pee. I go into the Gents. It's spotless. There's a pair of adjacent urinals, and a single cubicle. I opt for the privacy of a locked door. As soon as I'm safely inside, my head fills with the recollection of my blushing bolt-to-the-loo when I'd just clapped eyes on Dr M at Beecliffe.

I try to repeat my previous formula, telling myself again that now, I'm an adult. Don't feel like one. In fact, I feel like I did as a twelve-year-old choirboy, with a solo beckoning – the first verse of *Once in Royal David's City*, in front of a packed-out church. Christmas Eve, midnight mass. I'm all butterflies and cold sweat.

I'm sweating now. This time it's proper, powerful, grown-up sweat, accompanied by clammy palms, cold and sodden armpits and trickles running down my temples. I feel the urge to fart, but I don't dare.

Often – well, usually really – I feel that I am what others see. Someone physically large, powerful, prone to a touch of clumsiness, and stuck with a pair of giant mitts. But in this moment, it's all opposites. I feel shrunken, and diminished, like a weakling, a shrivelled little tortoise extracted from his shell.

I look at my watch. One minute to ten.

And now, suddenly, the only thought I have is that I mustn't be late.

Timid tortoise hares down the corridor, knocks on the door. The door opens in a couple of seconds. She lets me in, we both sit down in our chairs. I tell her that Jack is out of his box and is feeling really scared.

She says "OK, Jack, take your time and don't forget to breathe." And it's as if I needed to be reminded, so I take a few ravenous lungs-full, and then begin.

It pours out in a torrent.

A vision of a daughter who's a swaddled mummy. A crushing sense of guilt. A recognition of waves of anger which

196

have focussed onto Dr M. An eviscerating fear that Flo could be hurt by our attempts to help her. A stultifying terror of the cost of not trying. A bleak and haunting despair that I am beyond repair or redemption. An embarrassment that really, it's all just a conceited melodrama, a lot of fuss about nothing. The cascade carries these huge boulders. Wrecking balls which smash everything in their path.

She lets me go on. She shows me her ability to accept and absorb this deluge without drowning in it. Gradually, I slow down, and then eventually stop. I've talked myself to a standstill. We rest for a bit in the still of the aftermath. I look down at my hands. They're resting in my lap. They look reassuringly huge, which makes me smile.

She asks, "Now that you've said all of that Jack, how are you feeling"?

I tell her, "Dazed and confused." She says, "Yes." And after a short pause, she adds, "Me too. At the moment, I feel that I'm really struggling to hold in mind everything you've just said. But, as well as the struggle to hold on to all this information, and to absorb all the emotion you're unleashing, there's something else I'm aware of. It is the fact that you're here, of your own free choice. And that you have been able to avoid the temptation, and the trap, of retreating into silence."

She mentions Pandora's Box, and says that after all the chaos and confusion had burst out of it, the last thing to emerge was hope. She encourages me to recognise, and to identify with hope. I tell her that hope feels like a hug. I say, "A hug from a Mum, who can hold at bay the terrors of a world hell bent on havoc."

She smiles at me, and says, "There seems to be a lot of Mum stuff going on here. There's a Mum who can hug and protect you. A daughter you're claiming to have 'mummified'. You calling me 'Ma' at the end of yesterday's phone call. What do you think?"

I snap back with a brittle, "I don't know. You tell me. It's your interpretation. You explain it."

And she says, "What I'm wondering, Jack, is whether or not you have been able to ask your mother that big, frightful question. I can remember you saying to me, all that time ago, that you were never told about what actually happened when your father died. You said that you were away for the weekend, and were told that he'd suffered a fatal heart attack, but that no-one ever told you about the circumstances, the details. And that you'd always been too afraid to ask.

"So, Jack, what is it, the question you've never yet been able to ask your mother? What is the fear that keeps you locked in silence?"

No snappy response from me this time. My mind is enclosed by a deep, velvet blackness, and an empty silence...

Then eventually, the curtains open.

I say it all out loud, in a halting monotone, like a young kid reading from a book. Dull, flat, wrung dry from all feeling.

"I'm standing in the hall. We're almost ready to go. The cases have been packed and loaded in the boot. We're due to set off on the long drive to Cornwall for our summer holiday. Roy's away on Scout Camp. So, it's just me, Ma, Dad and the dog. Everything is stomach-knotted tense, which is the usual when we're on the brink of an outing. We never depart in peace.

"The dog, a big neurotic Alsatian, is leaking anxious nerviness all over the place. Dad opens the front door, and the dog bolts straight out into the garden, and ends up cowering round the back of the garage. Dad runs after her, grabs her by the collar, hauls her to the car and throws her in the back. He's shouting and swearing and purple-faced, with that vein throbbing vividly on his forehead. Ma runs out after him. She's incensed at his violence to the dog. She yells at him, 'For Christ's sake, stop it. Calm down, before you give yourself a heart attack." There's yelling and screaming from both of them. There's blood-curdling anger and exploding rage. It's unbearable. It feels heart-breaking.

"So, when he did actually have the heart attack, it begged that awful, unthinkable, unaskable question: Was there an almighty row which killed the old man? Did they both have a terrible fight which turned fatal?

"Mummy, did you cause the heart attack which killed my Dad?"

Dr M's voice comes to me. It sounds faint, remote, like she's talking through a blanket.

"Did you know, before, what the question was?"

I tell her I didn't have a clue.

She says, "Now that you do know, about your worst fear, do you think you'll be able to ask your Mother to simply tell you the circumstances of your father's death?"

I say I don't know, but I add that I've promised to phone her this weekend.

She says that our session will end soon, and then asks me if I feel there's anything else I want to say, or ask about, before I go. I tell her I don't think so. She says, "OK, but there is something which I want to say. Usually, I wouldn't use technical language or professional jargon with a client. But you are different, Jack. You have previous personal experience of psychotherapy and counselling. You have also studied psychology at university. And you now work at an Assessment Centre, alongside psychologists and psychiatrists, in an environment where the tools, and indeed the terms of this trade are central to your daily life. So, given all that, I want you to think about what is the meaning, technically, of the word transference. And, what it means to you, personally. If you wish to, Jack, you can give me your initial response right now. It's also something which I would urge you to reflect on between now and our next session."

I say, without any pause for serious thought, that transference is, as far as I understand it, pretty much what it says. It's about transferring stuff from its origin to somewhere, or sometime, or someone else. I say, for example, if I had a teacher at school who was an arrogant and opinionated and insensitive man, and then later, I met another male teacher, I might well assume that he too would be arrogant, insensitive and opinionated. I might, therefore, transfer the traits from one person to another. I add that the process would generally be unconscious, or at least subconscious. And I add, with a modestly triumphal flourish, that, "I believe that Freud referred to transference as the 'royal road to the unconscious', or something along those lines, and that it is the cornerstone to the psychotherapeutic process."

"There." I think to myself, smug, self-satisfied and waiting in warm anticipation for her to say, "Fantastic, well done, Jack. What a perfect understanding."

My expectation is half-fulfilled. What she actually does say is, "It looks as if you have a kind of external, technical understanding. But I wonder if you could apply the theory to the realities of your personal life experience?"

Ouch.

But, despite the pricking of my smug balloon, I still don't get it.

The walls of my defence system may have been breached here and there, but they're built on rock-solid foundations. They are built of granite, several feet thick. So, Dear Doc, how are you on the trumpet? Let's form a duet, a mini-brass-band. Blow up a storm, and watch those walls come a-tumbling down.

32

Sunday morning, nice day. Fizz, Flo and Marley are out in the back garden. I've told them I'll come out in a while, but I just have to make a phone call first. Don't say who I'm calling. Try to keep my voice light and bright, but Fizz gives me the look. I've been partially sussed. She sees that something's up, but she doesn't push it.

I dial the number. "Hello Ma, how are you?"

"Oh, hello Darling Boy. I'm just fine thank you. I had a lovely long chat with Fizz yesterday morning when you were out. Though I must say, she sounded a bit evasive about where you were and what you were up to. I got the impression she's a bit concerned about you – but I didn't want to pry." I say, "It's all a bit complicated. I'll tell you the whole story when I see you, over a large G&T, or two. Anyway, the abridged version for now is that the person I was seeing yesterday is a doctor – a psychiatrist in fact. She's someone I've got to know, and like, and trust, and we've asked her to help us with Flo. She's called Carol Mandrake. She works in the hospital in Newcastle."

Ma says, "Oh, I see," in a way that makes me feel like she probably doesn't see anything yet, but doesn't want to ask any questions which could be construed as fitting the not-really-any-of-my-business category. I take a deep breath, then take the plunge.

"The fact is Ma, I've got a question that I need to ask you. Probably should have asked it years ago, but never found the words, or the courage before." She says, "OK, Jack. I'm already sitting down. And I've got a cuppa in my hand so, what is it?"

I say, "What happened when Dad died?"

And she says, "He had a heart attack, a coronary thrombosis. I thought you knew."

I tell her, "Yes, I knew the heart attack bit. But I've never known anything of the story, the situation of what actually happened."

She says again, "Ah, I see." But her seeing this time is absolutely different. I can hear her taking a sip of tea, then a long breath, then another sip, followed by, "OK then, here goes.

You had gone off on your canoeing weekend. You left on the Friday afternoon. On Saturday morning, Daddy and I got up late, at about half past nine. He was exhausted. It had only been a couple of weeks since his mother, your Nanna, had died. He'd had all those ghastly trips up to Birmingham and back. Having to visit her in the hospital, then having to sort out the funeral. Doing it all by himself, no-one to help or share. Then, on top of all that, there'd been this really big business deal at work. It had been going on for months. It was worth millions, and it was his idea, his baby, and on that Friday, the previous day, they'd all signed the contracts. So he was delighted, excited and absolutely exhausted.

"Anyway, on the Saturday morning, after breakfast, we went to Egham, and we finally bought that lamp, the one I'd had my eyes on for ages, but thought was just too expensive. But Daddy said that he had clinched his biggest deal ever, so we just had to buy the lamp now. Said it was non-negotiable. Then we went to the Barley Mow for a snifter before lunch, but after only a few minutes in the pub, he said, 'Let's go home now', and as soon as we got back, he said, 'I'm going upstairs to lie down for a bit', which he did. Not like him at all, having a lie down in the middle of the day, but I thought nothing of it, apart from, 'He really must be worn out.'

"So, I started making lunch, and then Roy came home from rowing, and I said to him, 'Pop upstairs to tell Daddy that lunch will be ready in ten minutes.'

"Roy went half way up the stairs, called Daddy, but didn't get an answer, so he went into our room, and found him lying on the floor next to the bed. He yelled down to me, 'Ma, call an ambulance. Dad's having a heart attack.' I dashed into the dining room and phoned 999, and then ran upstairs to join Roy with Daddy. When I went into the room, Roy was giving Daddy mouth-to-mouth, and chest compressions, and he kept doing it till the ambulance arrived, and then they took over. Within a couple of minutes, they'd whisked him off to hospital.

"They all said that Roy couldn't have tried harder or done any more, but that, in all probability, Daddy had already died before Roy got into the bedroom.

"So, Darling boy, that's what happened."

I say, "Thank you for telling me, Ma. I'm so sorry if it's upset you, going through it again, all this time later."

And she says no, it's not been upsetting to tell me, though she can't understand why she didn't sooner.

And then, together, we both say, "Poor Daddy."

The great big sticking plaster has been peeled back a little further, revealing sore and tender skin. But I've been given a fresh blob of cool and soothing antiseptic cream, which I rub, gently, onto the newly exposed area, before going out into the garden to join my three girls.

They're all sitting on the big green and red plaid picnic blanket on the back lawn. Fizz is stroking Marley's head and gently tickling behind her ears. Flo's stroking her tail, from half-way downwards to the tip. Each time she gets to the end, Marley lifts it a few inches off the blanket, then lets it flop back down. Ted is sitting on the corner of the blanket watching proceedings with a wry smile. They see me walking towards them. Flo says, "Come and sit with us now, Daddy." I say, "Yep, coming." Marley sneezes, gives a short volley of tail-wagging, but otherwise seems pretty oblivious to my arrival.

Not so the other two. They've caught on to my mood. Fizz says, "Jack, are you all right?" And I say, "Yes. Really I am."

Flo says, "I think you're still too sad, Daddy. You look like you need to cry."

And I tell them both that I have every intention of crying, but that now I feel I will be able to cry with an easier heart, and that when the tears do flow, they will at last wash away the last dregs of that fear which used to eat away inside me.

Over the next fifteen minutes, I tell them the story of the phone call I've just had with Grandma. Fat tears do occasionally roll down my cheeks, but my voice holds. I try to explain why that particular conversation was delayed by all those years, and how much I feel relieved, and released, now it's done. They both say, "Poor Daddy." And after a bit of a pause, Flo says, "You can be better now." And we all sit together in the warm sunshine, in a haven of peace and quiet. Then Flo says, "Sometimes, some people just have to die, like Nancy did, they just can't help it. But now, maybe we've all got lucky, and Nancy can come home. Then we can all be together again."

Fizz and I both say, "That would be nice." And Flo says, "Will be. It will be lovely."

Marley wags her tail. First, she says "Woof," and then she says, "Woof, woof, woof", and we all say, "Come on then, walkies."

33

The first of Dr M's staff-training sessions had been scheduled for Thursday afternoon at 3.30. Dr Aveyleigh had made it crystal clear. The session was to be fully attended and was also to be enthusiastically received. No heckling, barracking or any form of piss-taking. The Centre's report writers in general, and the Big Deal Assessment show-case presenters in particular, would attend, learn, offer their sincere appreciation and subsequently demonstrate their new understanding. Three-line whip. No abstentions. For me, this was not a problem – at least from the perspective of my having a genuine interest in the subject matter and an urge to learn more about it. There was, of course, the other hand, which held an anticipation of embarrassment, that it might all feel a bit too close to the knuckle, that boundaries of privacy and confidentiality could be stretched, tested and, God forbid, maybe breached. However, I was pretty much a minority of one, and well outside the cosy consensus of most of my colleagues, the nutshell version of which was, "Why the hell do I have to give up my precious time in order to sit and listen to some bloody shrink wittering on about theories which are irrelevant, ludicrous, or both? All just to please Dr Bloody Aveyleigh. Bollocks."

In comparison to that lot, my enthusiasm was a puny weakling up against this full-to-the-brim bully of sulky dissent. So as well as feeling worried for myself, I was also full of anxiety on Dr M's behalf. But I'd never previously seen her working with a group, and maybe I'd presumed that her powers of engagement were confined to the privacy of individual close encounters.

There were about a dozen of us, all sitting around the great big table in the Case Conference room. Our orders were to be there early. We had obediently complied. She arrived at 3.30, precisely. She walked in, looked at us all, looked pointedly at the table, and said, "Oh dear!" and then asked if it would be possible to move it to the side of the room, so that we could sit together in a circle. She said that the table made it all feel a bit too stiff and formal for her, and that what she hoped for was a setting which would encourage everyone to relax and take part – more naturally and comfortably. There was a bit of lightly veiled grumbling, and one stage-whispered comment about it being a shame if Dr M didn't like it too stiff – which I saw her register and file, though she refrained from any response. Anyway, after a couple of minutes, we were duly reconfigured in the circle, though still well short of being relaxed.

Then she got to work. She started by saying that she believed that some, if not all of those assembled for the training had been press-ganged into it, which, from her point of view, made for a less than perfect start. She said that her work as a psychiatrist often required her to respond to a range of negative emotions – such as hostility, resentment, scepticism and anger – and that she expected that all of those feelings were in the room with us now. She also said that she hoped that some of us, at least, would also be feeling elements of curiosity about, and potential interest in what she might have to say, and that this potential was her chosen starting point.

She said that she knew we all worked with teenagers who presented us, frequently, with challenging actions and gruesome attitudes, and that it was both easy and tempting to denigrate and dehumanise the clients as differing varieties of monsters, wastes of space or assorted scum.

Then she added that she knew that many, if not all, of us were parents, that she was confident in her expectation that we would have tender, loving and protective feelings towards our children – most especially when they were babies – and that the difficult and dangerous teenagers with whom we worked started their lives as innocent babies too, but in their cases, their families, and the world in which they grew up had failed to provide the love, protection and care they needed to develop properly as humans who could love and be loved. Then she said that adolescence is, in a way, like a second chance at childhood, that it's a period of change, growth and potential, and that it offers the best, in fact the only realistic, chance these kids will have to acquire the insights and understandings which will enable them to develop, albeit belatedly, into adults whose lives can be OK – for themselves and those they live with. Then she paused for breath.

Not bad for openers, I thought. She breathed, so did the rest of us. Deep, serious breaths. Looks were exchanged. Hostility and resentment waned a bit whilst interest and connection waxed. Everyone's attention was strongly focused on her, and she knew it and used it. Ice was definitely broken. After a short pause for a few more deep breaths all round, she invited us all to think about any personal experiences we had of being with very young children, or indeed brand-new babies. Of the dozen there, ten were men – all but one already fathers, and the remaining one's wife was pregnant. The two women, both newish members of staff, were teachers, thirtyish, career-focused and currently child-free.

Having given us a few moments for private reflection, she asked us if we would briefly share some of our thoughts and personal experiences relating to babies with whoever was sitting next to us, so we did. And the room hummed with quietly exchanged memories of hospital bedsides and serene midwives, of confirmed atheists who suddenly resorted to the use of prayers and thanksgivings, of grown men shedding tears, and the fragile miracle of new lives entering the world. The room was filled with a powerful and protective tenderness.

Cynicism and resentment were, for the moment, gone. Dr M asked us all to take conscious note of our feelings, and to acknowledge the reality that one thing we all share in common is that we start our lives is as vulnerable, totally dependent creatures. She asked if anyone would blame a tiny baby for crying, or consciously deny it help and comfort. She asked us to consider the possibility that an infant's tears, or a toddler's furious tantrum, or a teenager's screaming tirade are all aspects of behaviour whose purpose is to communicate our feelings or needs to others, and that when such communication is ignored, or misunderstood, or consciously thwarted, we should expect trouble.

She said that she has no doubt that we are all familiar with trouble, and the way that trouble is created and expressed by extremely difficult and dangerous teenagers. And then she said that, rather than spending too much time on the familiar territory of adolescents' dysfunctional behaviours, she proposed instead that we shift our attention backwards, to consider the normal trials and tribulations of infancy and early childhood.

She said that there are times when such trials are unremitting horrors. That these trials can lead to the poor kids who endure them suffering from terrible miscarriages of justice, resulting in these victims emerging with the most unjust and undeserved consequences, which can then turn into harsh and unwarranted punishments. For some, literally, life sentences are imposed, from which there is scant hope of reprieve or redemption. She paused briefly, gathering her thoughts whilst still holding our attention, before adding, "And the worst of it is, these innocents often do succeed in convincing themselves that they are in fact guilty as charged, and from there, it's only the shortest of steps from being a victim to becoming a perpetrator."

And then, "Perhaps at this point, we might take a short break for a cup of tea." So, with the exception of Dr M and one of the teachers, everyone immediately lights up their cigarettes, or in two cases, their pipes, and we all greedily suck clouds of smoke into eagerly awaiting lungs.

There's a bit of general milling about. I see, with relief, that Dr M is engaged in chatting with the non-smokers, and I find I have something urgent to discuss with Ken Kaminsky, who happens to be far removed and safely ensconced in a corner. I don't really have anything I want to talk with Ken about. It's more a case of using him as a shield against the prospect of a direct and public encounter with Dr M. Anyway, after five minutes, she does a touch of significant throat-clearing, says we have only half-an-hour left, and asks us if we can continue. Within a few moments, and with just a bit of muted grumbling, we do.

She re-starts by saying that she now wants to return to those nearly new babies. She says that she believes many people subscribe to a myth, which holds that babies come into the world, not only with absolutely smooth bottoms, but also with absolutely innocent, and pure, and harmless attitudes. She says that such a view does not fit comfortably with her personal experience as a mother, or with her professional experience as a psychiatrist. She says, "There are many differing theories about what might be described as 'normal' in children's development. You may be relieved to hear that I am not going to spend much time exploring competing theoretical paradigms or perspectives. But I am going to say something about the work of one child psychotherapist in particular, a woman called Melanie Klein.

"Firstly, let me be absolutely clear. I am by no means a disciple of Dr Klein, nor do I believe in everything she taught or advocated. In fact, I think that some of her beliefs are incoherent, if not downright crazy. However, one of her core concepts is something in which I do wholeheartedly believe – something I just feel in my bones to be true. It is this. That aggression is an inherent and absolutely necessary aspect of being human. Aggression is not merely a set of learned behaviours. It is not an unfortunate symptom of poor parenting, or a sign of a deviant personality, or an expression of individual pathology. Aggression is a universal, and a vital part of our humanity. And what's more, infantile aggression cannot be avoided, and needs to be understood rather than denied or repressed. For infants to experience and express fury, rage and outrage is every bit as important for their healthy development as it is that they should experience love and tender nurturing. These notions stand at the heart of Klein's beliefs, and for me, they stand as foundational truths." A short pause, a sip of water, and then, "In fact, Klein goes further, by proposing that it is normal, in fact unavoidable, for the infant to experience feelings of persecution, to believe that significant care-givers – which usually means the infant's mother, not only persecute, but at times actually intend to kill, through the simple act of failing to immediately satisfy the infant's demand for food or care or comfort. And the theory is not just one way. It is not only that the powerless infant may fear being killed by the powerful adult. For Klein further holds that the infant will at times harbour murderous thoughts towards the mother, and indeed that the infant's fantasy of being possessed with omnipotent powers can magically transmute such thought into reality. So she suggests that infants can, in a sense wish for the death of those close to them and at the same time believe that such a wish can come true.

Dr M says she's not sure that she is fully on board with Klein here. What's more, the atmosphere in the room suggests that the Beecliffe Assessment Report writers are well short of complete conversion to full-blown Kleinianism themselves.

As for me, I'm in a separate little world of my own, far, far, away from the interest of report writing. I'm looking at Little Flo, who seems to be almost crushed with sadness and regret. She's said just six words. "Sorry Nanny, I didn't mean to."

Now, there's a thing.

34

After the first session that Flo and I had with Dr M, I asked a couple of times, "So, Flo, how are you feeling about going back to see Dr Mandrake again next Tuesday?" And she just said, "Fine," in a way that sounded relaxed and uncomplicated and no big deal. I decided not to push it. And nor did Fizz, whose approach, though a bit more subtle, still elicited the same kind of a not-much-comment response.

But what Fizz and I did notice independently, and then confirmed to each other in a couple of late-night chats, was the dramatic change in Flo's manner and relationship with Ted. In fact, Ted too used to be one of a pair – Ted and Ed. They were similar, though not quite identical, and were a first-birthday present to the twins from Grandma. Right from their initial encounter, Flo really took a shine to Ted, and, pretty much from the moment they met, they were inseparable, the normal configuration being for Flo to hold Ted in her left hand, snuggled in her neck, so it looked as if he was constantly whispering in her ear. If Flo needed to use both hands for anything, she'd tilt her head, and shrug her left shoulder, like grownups do with a phone. And, pretty much for Ted and Flo – a pair of quiet, virtually Siamese twins – that used to be it. Until our car journey home from that first session, when Ted had become independent, active and animated, engaged in conversations with Flo – at times in agreement, but also voicing alternatives, or even showing downright dissent. That was the stuff I glimpsed in the rear-view mirror, and it was the stuff that was growing and developing at home.

Flo and Ted were no longer just a pair of silent allies and furtive co-conspirators. They were openly talking, and laughing and, now and then, arguing. Late one Friday night, Fizz and I were talking about Ted's newly discovered voice, and were both agreeing that it was probably a good thing and an encouraging sign.

Fizz offered me the joint that she'd just rolled and lit, and I said, "No thanks, not tonight." And she said, "My God, Jack, are you alright? Do you need a doctor?" And I said, "Yes, I'm fine, and no, I don't need a doctor, I'm seeing one in the morning, and that's why I want to keep a clear head!" And Fizz said, "Well I'm blessed," quoting my Ma, and sounding just like her. And I said, "Me too. Blessed, that is." And, in the softly cushioned safety of that moment, I thoroughly believed it as the simple and absolute truth.

35

It's Saturday morning, five to ten, and I'm back in that corridor, thirty yards short of Dr M's door. I've just been for a pee, which I managed comfortably using the urinal this time, and, generally, I'm sweat-free and feeling calm. Well, calm-ish. And I'm curious. There's a distinct and separate part of my mind which is watching these entire goings on. I get the image of myself as some white-coated scientist, peering down a microscope, observing with cool fascination some bits of me – magnified, illuminated and semi-detached from context.

Naturally, I've still got some butterflies flapping about –

but, just now, the butterflies are in the wings, they're not centre-stage. I'm outside her door, raising my left index knuckle, about to go knock-knock, at which precise moment she opens the door, which gives me a feeling of vertigo, falling through a solid which had suddenly turned into an empty space. We both seem to be startled by the expected, which had somehow got a second ahead of itself. We take our seats. She invites me to take a moment. I look at her, and, with instant and enormous relief, recognise the reality that it's safe for me to say anything and everything which comes to mind.

I look at myself, from outside myself, from a couple of feet above my left shoulder. Jack-in-the-chair fidgets a little, looks at his hands, clears his throat, sees the possibility of the opening few words of a sentence, sees the opportunity of taking the opener in different directions – towards alternative conclusions – but I can't decide on the end point, and therefore can't make the start. Jack-in-the-air watches all this, at first like the white-coated scientist, but soon becomes softened with a wry smile. The scientific white-coated Jack-in-the-air feels pangs of compassion for the stuttering lump-in-the-chair, and in doing so, joins him.

I say, "I feel as if there are three of us here in the room. There's you, and there's me, and there's a part of me which is watching the proceedings, kind of from the outside." Dr M says, "How interesting. Is this a new thought, or something which has occurred to you before?" And I say, "Not entirely new, but just now it feels more vivid and powerful." She says, "Is this what you want to focus on at the moment?" And with that question, Jack-in-the-chair realises that Jack-in-the-air ain't there.

But my Ma is.

Ma is in the here and now, and, magically, at the same time, she's there at home, exactly as I'd pictured her, sitting in her dining-room, cup of tea on the coaster on the table in front of her, talking to me on the phone, telling me the answer to the question about Dad and his dying.

So that's the story I tell Dr M, and she simply absorbs it all. Like blotting paper, sucking up my little puddle of tears. As I'm sitting in the peaceful aftermath of telling this tale, another thought comes to mind, a fresh one. White coat. Me in a white coat. A part of me, becoming, what, one of them? Now I'm a turncoat? Siding with, sliding into the enemy? I run all this stuff past Dr M. Of course, she's heard all about the white coats before.

It feels as though she's holding up a mirror, so that I can see my reflection. I watch myself and notice there's only one of me. I reflect on my reflection, enjoying the pun. As the imagined mirror-image recedes, Dr M re-enters present reality with a question. "Jack, last week I brought up the issue of transference, and invited you to reflect on it, not just as a theoretical construct, but also as an aspect of your experience. Would you like to share any thoughts about this with me now?"

I asked her straight, "Do you play the trumpet?"

And then I told her what I'd been thinking, that I'd built impregnable defences around myself, which I then re-imagined as the walls of Jericho. I wanted her to be Joshua, and to blow that horn. "How interesting," she said, again, the second time in the session. In fact she went on, saying, "When I was a teenager, I had an overwhelming passion for music. I started to learn to play the clarinet, and knew I had a genuine talent. I saw myself as a professional musician, playing everything from the classics to jazz. But my parents would not allow, let alone encourage my interest in music. They insisted that I follow the family tradition in studying medicine. My only act of mild rebellion was to become a psychiatrist rather than a surgeon."

So, I told her, "As my mother would say, 'Well, I'm blessed'."

And she says, "Please excuse my digression. I asked you about the transference issue, and your answer, it seems to me, was about defences. Do you feel that the two are connected in your mind?" I ask, a bit abrasively, what she's trying to suggest. And she says, quite neutrally, that she is trying not to make any suggestions, but to ask what she hopes will prove to be relevant questions. "Mmm," I say, with lingering attitude. Then I have a patch of feeling thoroughly blank. Really empty-headed. I've gone from two of me to nobody at home. Somehow, it feels as if I'm looking at the blank, and daring it. Staring it out. Who's going to blink, blank? We sit together, wrapped in quiet. Not knowing.

Then, Dr M moves. Her hands go from her lap to the arms of her chair. Her feet go from evenly placed on the floor to crossed at the ankle. This movement creates a little eddy of air, which carries over to me a faint, but distinct whiff of her perfume. Her scent is, as always the absolute essence of my Ma. A substantial presence of Ma.

I feel there's a tantalising but impossible prospect of a hug. If only, that hug could have made all the troubles in the world evaporate. It could have been the enticing antidote to all those

221

comments, those injunctions of: "Don't make a fuss," or "Least said…", and here's the conflation, of the real and present Dr M, who does want me to say anything and everything that matters, to give voice to all hurt, but a Dr M who sure as hell ain't able to give me that hug.

All of these ideas arrive in my head simultaneously – a complete can full of worms, with the lid off, and in a few rushed and jumbled sentences, I'm able to find the words which are just about good enough to describe this wriggling, intertwined heap of thought and feeling.

Having said all that out loud, I have a physical sensation which I recognise and relish.

This is the scene. It's after I've played in a rugby match. I'm in the bar. I quickly down a pint, and immediately feel horribly bloated. But then I belch, long, loud and luxuriously. Then I joyfully realise that sense of absolute comfort and wellbeing which accompanies the replacement of a tight discomfort with the delicious empty space inside.

I share this image with the Dr M. I say, "Pardon me." She says, "Granted." Then she adds, "It's almost time to end the session. But before we do, I'd like to give you a direct quotation from Melanie Klein. She said, 'with pining for what has been lost or damaged by hate comes an urge to repair.' So, in order to repair something, one needs not only the urge to do so, but some space to work in. I feel you now have both. Which makes me feel really happy."

And I say, "Really? Happy?" She says, "Yes."

I say, "Oh." And then, "Me too."

36

Flo and I stand there, outside Dr M's door, hand in hand. She says, "Are you ready?" And I say, "Yes", and she knocks on the door, with a rat-a-tat-tat, just like the doctor did when he visited Polly's dolly who was sick, sick, sick.

The door opens on Flo's final tat, and Dr M greets us with a warm smile. "Hello, I'm pleased to see you, come in," which we do, Flo going straight to her chair. She sits back, her legs dangling over, swinging gently a few inches above the floor. Dr M and I take our seats. Flo takes the initiative. She says, "I'm going to tell you, before you ask. Ted isn't coming today. He's staying at home, so he can be with Mummy and Marley. I'll tell him everything later. Now you can have my under-vided attention."

Dr M says she thinks this is an excellent start, and asks Flo if she remembers anything particular about our last session together. Flo says "Definitely, lots. At the end, you showed me your toy cupboard, and said next time I can choose. Now it's next time, and I want to play with dolls."

Dr M says, "OK, you can."

Flo says, "Do you have enough for one each for all of us?" And Dr M says, "Yes, I'm sure we can manage that." And Flo asks her, "What will you do, while I play with the dolls? Will you play with us too?" And Dr M says, "Not exactly. But I will watch, and listen as carefully as I can. And sometimes I'll probably ask you to explain if I don't understand." Flo says, "That's OK, but what will Daddy do?" And Daddy says, "I'm going to draw a picture."

So, that was the deal. We would all start at the same time, just as soon as we'd got our respective bits of equipment sorted out.

I'm keeping a furtive eye and ear on Flo, who strikes me, in that moment, as something of an aspiring control freak. She's being regally bossy towards Dr M, saying, "Right. Now we need at least four dolls, for Mummy, Daddy, Nancy and me. Then another one for you, if you do want to join in. And we'll have another little one for the baby, in case she's not going to be Nancy again this time. Then maybe a few more for just-in-cases."

Dr M says she's got plenty of dolls in her drawer, and should she bring them all out for Flo to choose, and Flo says, "Certainly." But then she appears puzzled, and slightly anxious as she surveys the collection of figures in front of her.

She says, "What if some of them aren't the right colour?"

Dr M asks her what she means, and Flo says, straight away, "Well, in our family, everyone's got different coloured skins." Dr M says that's true and she had noticed. Flo seems to be chewing this one over in her mind for a moment, then gives a lightweight sigh, followed by a shrug and announces that, "Really, it doesn't matter. We'll just have to pretend."

I had been provided with a large sheet of white drawing paper and a tin with twenty-four Lakeland coloured pencils, all freshly sharpened. I'm hovering, pencil in hand, but really, all I want to do is watch and listen to Flo and Dr M. I flirt with a brief fantasy of being safely stuck behind an observation window, unseen but all-seeing.

Then Flo catches me, red-handed, in mid-stare. "Daddy! What are you doing? You have to make your picture while we're playing with these dolls. No peeping. That's the promise."

I tell her sorry, and yes, she's right, and right, I promise. Then I sit there, gazing at the big blank sheet, and feeling empty. And just a little bit sick.

Slightly sick, and increasingly weird. Half awake. Half aware. Watching as the dream sequence gradually unfolds. I become vaguely conscious of myself picking up one of the pencils and beginning to draw. I don't feel personally involved, let alone responsible. I watch the outline as it emerges under its own volition. It becomes a match-stick man, who then acquires a pair of enormous hands. My head-voice gives a snort of derision, sneering, "No prize for guessing this one." I feel as if I've jumped from being a sneaky Peeping Tom and morphed into Narcissus, creating the form for his own reflection.

I watch as the picture appears. The sickly feeling has gone, pretty much. It's replaced with the self-absorbed fascination of watching the outlines as they're acquiring their definition and substance. Better still, whilst the picture is busy defining itself on the paper, my mind is reviving a hitherto lost piece of memory…

I'm four years old. I've just had my birthday, and I'm about to use my present for the very first time. It's a painting book. "Just paint with water, to make the colours and the pictures magically appear."

New picture at hand, old pictures in mind. Occasional words drift across from Flo's intermittent monologue. Disconnected. Barely decipherable. Allowing me to dot-to-dot them into my sense of her meaning.

A little later, I'm nearly done. My picture looks like it's an authentic piece of untalented junior school artwork.

There's a big-handed ham-fisted me, standing under a dark and dreary cloud. My eyes are sightless crosses, mouth an upside-down curve, crudely stitched shut. I'm standing knee deep in a puddle. The black cloud hovers, just above head height. There's a sharp yellow flash of lightning which penetrates the cloud, illuminating one half of the picture below.

A small character, a mini-matchstick person, touches my hand with an outstretched finger.

There's a matchstick dog with a wagging tail.

And there's a matchstick mum.

I am standing entirely under the dark shadow. The little one, touching my hand, stands on the borderline of brightness and gloom. The dog and the mum are bathed in brightness.

The cloud is an angry scribble of black and blue. It's thick and heavy, like an aching bruise. The puddle is dark and deep. The rain is like stair-rods. The lightning is the only source of light.

I'm just about to announce that I've finished, when I tune in to the voice of Dr M, who is asking Flo something, though her question is indistinct. Flo's answer, however, is absolutely crystal. She says, "Well, Nancy couldn't come back, not before, 'cos we weren't even allowed to say her name. So I couldn't tell her that I was sorry, or that I didn't mean to."

Then Dr M says, "Is there anything which you would like to say to Nancy now?"

Flo doesn't lift her gaze from the collection of dolls on the floor, but, after a little pause and a big sigh, she says, still without looking up, "Well, now it's easy. Now I can say anything I want. Now I can talk to Nancy all the time. Even out loud."

37

I had always thought of Nicky as being absolutely unattainable – an impossible prospect – who made me feel that I was all of her exact opposites. I thought that she was delicate, graceful and assured whereas I was overgrown and awkward, all blushing fingers and thumbs. Her balance and beauty were the polar opposite to my general oversized shambles. So, although I had this moonstruck longing for her, although I literally and hopelessly dreamed about her, I held the sure conviction that I was not good enough for her – that I'd never deserve so much as a second glance.

So, it had come as a simple confirmation of my hopeless prospects when I met up with her at the youth club and saw that she and Kev had become an item. Then later, even after I'd heard that the golden couple had split up – Kev's version being that he'd got bored with her, and then casually dumped her – even then it just convinced me that she'd find some new trophy boyfriend, and despite bits of previous wishful thinking, never imagined myself as a realistic prospect.

But then, Friday night, 31st March, ten to seven. The eve of my fifteenth birthday. The doorbell rings, dog barks, Ma says, "Who on earth could that be? Jack, go have a look please." I grumble, go to open the door, and there she is, giving me a sheepish smile and a brief glance before returning her intense gaze to her shoes. She says, "Sorry to just turn up on your doorstep, but I felt like I had to see you. Can I come in?" And I say, "Sure."

But before she even gets through the door, Ma calls from the kitchen, "Who is it, Jack?" and I say, "It's Nicky." And immediately, I change from the notion of inviting her in to the decision of walking her home. I grab my coat from the banister, and call over my shoulder, "I'll be back in a while." And I bundle the pair of us out of the house as quick as I can. No backwards glance.

It's quite warm, mostly clear-skied, with an occasional bit of white fluff. The clocks have just gone forward, so the later light is a surprise – a hopeful taste of summer–to-come. We walk out through the open front gates, turn right, head up Bagshot Road, through the village, towards The Green. There's a ragbag of confusion in my head – a bunch of questions all competing with each other, vying for front stage, cancelling each other out, resolving into a stalemate of silence.

Nicky stays quiet too, though she seems a lot more cool and calm than I feel. She breaks our silence after a long few minutes by saying, "I suppose you've heard then," to which I reply with a nondescript bit of a grunt, before she continues, "About me and Kev, splitting up." I say that I didn't know, and Nick says that's not what Kev told her, so I say that all I meant was that I didn't know what had really happened, or why, and Nick says, "I see," and we then walk the rest of the way to The Green in a dark cloud of wordless quiet which feels forlorn and immovable.

We sit together at the edge of The Green, on a bench, watching the dregs of a spectacular sunset fade into monochrome as the first stars come into view. At last, Nicky says, "Sorry, Jack, maybe this was a bad idea," and I just about manage to squeeze out a three-word reply of, "Don't be sorry," before clamming up again. But Nick seems like she wants to talk, and she's able to, and over the next half-hour the whole story pours out, stuttering and jagged at first, then in an absolute torrent. How Kev had pretended, at first, to be so nice, so considerate, such a gentleman. How suddenly all of that stuff was revealed to be load of bullshit, how he'd lied, and bragged to everyone at the youth club, saying that Nicky was "an absolute raving nympho." How he'd nicked a bottle of vodka from his dad's booze cabinet, gone to her house when he knew her parents were out, got her blind drink, shagged her, and left her crying in a crumpled bloody heap. And never bothered, later, to find out if she was OK. Never phoned. Not a word. Nothing.

Nothing, in fact, till earlier this evening, when she was walking home and just happened to bump into Kev, who just happened to be strolling along hand-in-hand with Sally. Kev's face was pasted with a nasty, cruel sneer. He said, "You all on your own then, Nicky? Got no friends now?"

But Nick says, "No, not true. Actually, I'm going round to Jack's, right now. And he's a better friend, and a better bloke than you'll ever be, Kevin." And having said she was going to see me, she just had to do it, which was how come she'd turned up on my doorstep.

I'm sitting there, having just heard the girl I've been infatuated with since the age of nine, tell me that I'm a truer friend and a better bloke than my best mate, who used to be her boyfriend, could ever be.

And, in fact, that my best mate had conned and forced Nick into having sex with him, and generally behaved like a slime-ball.

I just don't know what to believe. Definitely don't know what to make of the whole thing. But what I do know is that I'm sitting with Nicky on a bench, under a sky full of glistening stars, with a sliver of moon climbing above the tree line, and she's just taken hold of my hand, and she's saying, "It's true, you know, I do feel safe with you, Jack. I know you'd never do a thing to hurt me." And I tell her that, for absolute sure, is true, and there's nothing I could want more than to just take care of her, and there's nothing I'd want in return, no price to be paid, and then she gives me a light kiss on the cheek, and I turn my head, and we kiss each other on the lips – as if by accident at first – and then, seriously, on purpose, and I dissolve into mindless, thoughtless, total bliss.

Later, we pull apart. Come up for air. She smiles, but it's brief. Her smile soon turns to a flickering frown, and a hesitant question. "Jack, how come we never see you at the youth club now? Nobody's seen you for weeks. Have you gone off us all, or are you turning into some kind of hermit?"

I can't get away with saying nothing, so I mumble, "It's 'cos of my dad."

She looks blank. Doesn't say anything at first. Nor do I. We're stuck again, in a head-lock of silence. And then, it's as if her whole body is hit by the awful realisation. And she says, "Oh shit, Jack. Oh shit." And I say "Yeah," without having a clue but just feeling suddenly sick and scared. Then she tells me:

"Everyone was there, all of the usual crowd, at the club. Then Kev appears, and he's full of crap, loads of bragging bollocks, in the middle of which, for no apparent reason, he comes out with, 'Anyway, we probably won't be seeing Jack here for a while,' and we all go, 'Why not?' and he says, 'Cos his dad's just died of a heart attack.' And Sally, my mate Sally, and I both thought he was only saying it for some kind of sick, dramatic effect, and we told him so, and then we walked off."

Nicky says that it had hardly crossed her mind since, and that when she did think of it, she only saw it as evidence to prove how screwed-up Kev must be, to make up something like that. Never thought, for a moment, it could've been true. I say, "Yep Nick, it is true." And then add, "Sorry."

She holds my face in her hands. She's still, and she's silent. But then, big fat tears start to roll down her cheeks. I try to wipe them away, at first with my thumbs. But I worry that my hands

232

are too rough, that they'll scratch her skin. So, instead, I lick away her tears, then start kissing her face, all over. Again and again, saying, "It's all right, Nick, honest, it's all right."

Later, we went to the off licence. I had money, five pounds in a birthday card from Auntie Audrey, already opened and pocketed. I got a flagon of Bulmer's cider and a bottle of Smirnoff vodka which we took to the kids' park, where we sat, getting hysterical on the swings, wild and dizzy on the roundabout, taking a sip each, in turn, till the bottles were done and we were well and truly and helplessly pissed. Then, at maybe about three in the morning, we sneaked back into my house. Nicky slurred, "What about your Mum?" and I told her not to worry, 'cos Ma was now on a special diet every night – sleeping pills washed down with gin. And so we simply sneaked in, crept upstairs, into my room, into bed.

And all that lot added up to the necessary and sufficient causes to create the perfectly poisonous cocktail. So, when Ma came into my room later that morning bearing my birthday gift, all three of us got one hell of a shock, which turned, irrevocably, into a gut-wrenching epic of a nightmare.

I think that, probably, Nick and I had done it, the sex stuff, or at least tried to do it, the moment we'd drunkenly fallen into bed. Neither of us could remember if we actually had. But definitely, definitely I wanted – and it seemed Nick wanted – to do it, either again or for the first time. There and then. Despite the fact that we both had pounding headaches, furred-up and dried out tongues, despite feeling dreadful and dizzy, none of that was as powerful as the urge.

The urge won. Hands down. Hands up. Holding hands. Hands caressing and exploring, soothing, stroking. All over. Everywhere. Not just hands. Every conceivable bit. Inconceivable bits too.

Apart from lots of wordlessly biting my lip and holding my breath, there were a few moments when I said stuff. I said that I thought she was the most gorgeous thing in the world, that I would never do anything to hurt her, that all I wanted was to take care of her and keep her safe. And Nicky said that she did feel safe with me, and knew she could trust me, and had just, suddenly, realised how much she fancied me. In that early morning soft light, she said all those things. Not only said, but wanted to show, to prove. We'd been lying side by side then she rolled over, her knees straddling my hips, her hands on my chest, the top sheet and eiderdown falling to the floor. That was the precise moment when we heard the tap-tap on the door. I looked up. Nicky turned round to look over her shoulder. Our eyes locked with Ma's. All three of us must have looked like lame actors doing shock and horror in a silent movie.

Then the scene went slo-mo, but no longer silent. The volume had been turned right up. Ma let go of the tray. Toast, coffee, juice, neatly wrapped present, all hit the carpet with a loud and messy crash.

Ma's words were few but unforgettable.

"It's been hardly any time since your father died! You would not have dreamed of behaving this way if he was still alive. Now, get that slut out of my house. Immediately. I never want to see her again. And right now, Jack, I can't stand to look at you either. So get out. Both of you." All of which was ringing-in-your ears shouting. Then there's a pause, and a couple of deeply shuddering breaths, before a final, whispered, "Allow me my misery in peace."

It took us maybe a minute. A silent scramble of getting dressed – no time to wash, clean teeth, not even a pee. No words between us, none to Ma either. She by then had retreated to the unapproachable confine of her locked bedroom.

Once out of the house, we more or less retraced our steps of the night before, ending up on the same bench by The Green. The size and strength of our hangovers was enough, by itself to reduce us to a pair of slack-mouthed mutes. We were crushed by the weight of all that unspeakable stuff, everything that had happened in between the then and there which had started in the blaze of last night's magical sunset to the here and now of this morning's hopeless gloom.

So, no tender touch or reassurance. No gentle whispered thanks. No respite from gut-wrenched hurt, no glimmer of hope ahead. The one and only thing in my mind was the cracked record's refrain of, "But I'm not sorry. I'm glad." But I didn't have a clue about how I could possibly explain what I meant. I was stuck, locked into the thought that Nicky was sitting there, right next to me, thinking to herself, "Twice on the trot. With two different blokes. Same recipe. Getting pissed and getting screwed." And I couldn't stop myself from believing that my fears were in fact Nicky's only thoughts. I was stuck in the corner. Glum and dumb.

The longer we sat there, the worse it felt. Both of us made

pathetic and faltering attempts to talk, but they all petered out with dismal stutterings of, "That's not what I meant to say," and a miserable sigh and a head-in-the-hands, "Oh shit."

In the end, Nicky said, "I have to go home. My Mum and Dad are away and my brother's supposed to be looking after me and I don't want him to come looking." This was her only coherent statement of the morning. And all I could muster as a reply was, "OK. Sorry." And she said, "Me too." And that was it, no kiss, no touch. No farewell. No fucking hope. Just ashes, a mouth full of ashes.

I really did think that that was as bad as it could get. Thought I'd plumbed the depths, reached rock bottom. In the space of a few hours, I'd gone from being the absolutely hopeless outside contender, to having and holding the girl of my dreams, and then telling and showing her that I loved her – always had, always would – and believing for a moment that she could even love me back. I'd just done the whole trip, from wildly elated drunken euphoria, through the sudden, ghastly crash of a tea-tray, through the maelstrom of Ma's grief-fuelled outrage and then, smashing on the razor-rocks of a lethal hangover, drowning in guilt and if-onlys.

For sure, all that stuff was seriously bad. But, without a whisker of doubt, it got worse. It turned into the stuff of a horror which made me yearn to get back to my life as it was on that birthday morning.

For one thing, miserable and horrible as it was when Nicky and I went our silent, separate ways from the green, I didn't believe in that moment that we'd never see each other again. But the brutal fact was that the last I ever saw of Nicky was her walking across the green, past the Barley Mow, turning right. Gone. Disappeared.

I spent a few days at home, locked away in my bedroom, trying to find the courage to phone her and failing every time. I'm not sure which felt the more frightening: the idea of Nicky's mum, or dad or brother picking up the phone, and then me saying who I am, and asking, "Please may I talk to Nicola?" and thinking that I'd have a complete melt-down if I was in any way challenged about my background or intentions. Or, even more terrifying, what if Nicky picked up the receiver herself. Either way phoning was too frightening for words – and pretty fucking pointless for a speechless half-wit. So, instead, I decided I'd write a letter. Did write, in fact, dozens of starts, but absolutely failed to get beyond, "Dear Nicky, I'm writing/I want to write/I need to/I'm trying to…" Each attempt stalled on the opening, ground to a halt and was then screwed into a tight ball and flung towards the overflowing bin.

So, from me, nothing was said or sent. Nor received. Resounding silence, wall to wall. Though I did hear that, by the end of the summer term, Nicky failed to show up at school, and the rumour was that she'd moved down to Portsmouth to live with her Nan. But even that didn't feel like the end of all hope. I was still having these vivid dreams, day and night, in which Nicky and I met up again, and all our troubles simply disappeared and we held each other safe and sound.

But no.

No.

The absolute end came through our letterbox. Two items. The weekly local rag – *The Staines and Egham Gazette*, and a letter, hand-written, from Nicky. I immediately recognised her writing, and stood there, paralysed, dying to open the letter, but too scared.

I was in the hall. For some reason, I'd run down as soon as I heard the snap of the letterbox, despite the fact that it's something I usually just ignored. I picked up the paper and letter, then ran back upstairs, three at a time, bolted into my bedroom and locked the door. I took a couple of shaky breaths, sat down on the edge of my bed, dropped the paper to the floor – half-folded, headline facing up. I looked at the envelope. Just my name and address, nothing else. It felt heavy, as if there were a few pages inside.

I was blushing crimson. Sweat rolling down my face, trickling down my chest and back. I wiped my arm across my forehead, trying to mop my drenched brow with the short sleeve of my T-shirt. OK, I thought, maybe I'll just have enough courage to open the letter if I do it quick – right now. So I took a deep breath, which I held, but just as I was about to tear open the envelope, my gaze shifted to the floor. To the paper. To the headline, which shouted 'Local girl killed in scooter crash. Tragic accident or suicide?" And, visible below the headline before the type disappeared round the fold, were the first words of the story's opening.

"The body of a local girl, Nicola Donaldson, aged 16, was found…"

I dropped the letter, bent down to pick up and unfold the

paper and saw the story continuing down the left-hand column, to the bottom of the page, and next to it a picture of Nicky, looking pretty much as she did on that last day that I'd seen her. I stared at the picture then let the paper fall to the floor and just started to sob, quietly and gently. But I couldn't stop. Streaming tears, running snot, open-mouthed spit dribbling and splashing, forming puddles on the paper and the envelope beside it. I looked at the wet patterns which were forming, grimly fascinated. It took some time before my head and eyes cleared enough for me to return to the unbelievable nightmare of the blurb.

In fact, I only got to finish the front page. That was more than enough. It said that Nicky's body had been discovered by a dog-walker. She was lying in a crumpled heap, next to a Lambretta 125 scooter, evidently having crashed into the wall which edged the curve in the road. She wasn't wearing a crash helmet. There were no skid marks on the road. And, in the final sentence on the front page, "The subsequent autopsy revealed the fact that Nicola was three months pregnant." It said 'turn to page 6 for more details.' And I said, quietly, but out loud, "No. Fuck it. I've read enough. No more details." I picked up the envelope and the paper, put both together under the mattress, put on jeans and sandals, walked out of my bedroom, downstairs to the kitchen, lifted Ma's handbag from the table, took out her purse, removed a fiver, put the money and my door key in my pocket, walked out of the house and went straight to the off-licence.

I think it would have been about ten in the morning when I left. By half past, I'd started drinking, knocking it back with savage anger. By lunchtime, I passed out. As soon as I came round, I started again on the remains of the vodka. I can't give any kind of coherent account of what happened next. I was in the graveyard of St Jude's church. I remember doing a lot of shouting, a bit of pissing on gravestones and some lobbing of anything I could get my hands on at the stained-glass windows.

I suppose this bizarre spectacle had inspired some onlookers to call the police.

I saw him, the uniformed officer, walking towards me, inviting me to calm down. But I was in no mood. I was so full of rage and booze that there was no space or wish for calm.

He came right up to me. He was probably trying to put a friendly arm round my shoulder, which, unfortunately, I took to be an attempted head-lock. There was an unseemly tussle, which ended up with some of his arm around most of my neck. Which I objected to. I bit him. Sunk my teeth into his forearm. Which I imagine was when, and why, he whacked me over the head with his truncheon.

Which was when I went down and passed out, good and properly unconscious. For quite a while.

I do remember my first thought as soon as I came round. Despite the massive bruise on my head, the heaving waves of nausea, the smell of my piss-soaked jeans and the pitiful wish to regain unconsciousness, there was one bit of my mind which was cool and crystal clear. The voice inside my head recited, "Right. That's it. I am not saying a single word, not to any fucker, not about anything. My lips are sealed."

38

Friday evening, I volunteered to do tea: bangers, beans and mash. I had the kitchen to myself – apart from Marley, who sat in the corner looking hopeful. The girls were in the front room, the door ajar. I could hear snippets about dolls and babies and Dr M, but felt little temptation to seriously listen-in, thinking that Fizz would tell me later, and for now my mind could just relax and wonder. Whilst happily immersed in this state of being – as Pink Floyd would have it – comfortably numb, a couple of the bangers under the grill erupted in spurts of fatty flame. I pulled the grill-tray out, clumsily, and in doing so managed to dislodge two of the sausages which fell into the back corner of the top oven. I put the grill-tray down on the draining-board, then reached in to retrieve the fallen bangers, and in the process, succeeded in pressing the back of my hand onto the red-hot grill, giving it a serious sizzle.

Nasty. Ouch. I doused my hand under the cold water tap, then reached for the first aid basket to get the Germolene. A bit of a whispered, "Ow, fuck. Fucking hell, ow," followed by the application of a large cool blob of the pinky-white cream. Then a slow and shaky sit-down at the table, holding the injured hand by the wrist, giving it a gentle shake and long blows through pursed lips.

The smell of the Germolene triggered yet another childhood memory…

I'm four years old, and I'm belting along on my bike, stabilisers recently discarded, skidding round and coming off at the corner, and removing most of kneecap's worth of skin. Blobs of watery blood appeared, and the whole mess was patterned with painfully imbedded grit and gravel.

Back home, Ma did the repair job with warm wet cotton-wool, lightly Detolled, and a pair of tweezers. Then, once it was clean she applied a great dollop of Germolene, which seemed – miraculously – to replace the trembling sick-to-the-stomach pain with a feeling of calm relief.

This whole memory flared as a single scene in my head, but then it connected to subsequent images, stretched over a longer timeframe. Within a day or two of the scrape, a great crusty scab started to form. And a couple of days after that, the scab became an irresistible site for inspecting and scratching and picking. Round the edges, it revealed, with a bit of careful lifting, the miraculous formation of fresh pink skin beneath. But, pick too deep, and drops of blood would appear.

Every incident of scab-picking which Ma observed led to a telling-off. Apparently, this activity was, for some unspecified reason, not just prohibited but also somehow morally reprehensible. Picking was taboo. And, apparently, dangerous. It could lead to a permanent scar and a possible infection. But neither of these prospects reduced my overpowering urge to pick, which felt as irresistible as sneezing.

Then, abruptly, my lingering in memory lane was interrupted by the girls' arrival. Flo looked at me, and looked at my hand, and sighed with a mixture of sympathy and exasperation. She put her hands on her hips and said, "Oh Daddy, what have you gone and done to yourself now?"

So, together, we finished the cooking, and did the table-setting, squash-making, then the eating, then washing-up, "Not you Daddy. You mustn't get your hand wet. You just do the drying." After all of which, Fizz and Flo went off to do bath and bed.

As soon as they were out of the kitchen, I got straight back to my compulsive business of memory mining.

Where's that scab? Let me at it.

My mind feels like Marley on a walk in the woods. Suddenly unleashed, set free to sniff around, and search and wander.

Wounds and scabs.

Protective layers and tender insides.

These are the contents of my head.

Here's Flo. She's swaddled from head to toe. I'm holding the exposed end of a detaching bandage between my thumb and forefinger. She gives a twirl, spins like a slow-motion top, and the whole thing starts to unravel. The vision stays vividly real but grows increasingly impossible. Because the more the bandage is removed, the bigger the body inside becomes, slivers of flesh are glimpsed behind and between the unwinding layers of bandage. Creamy, white flesh. Strands of hair emerge, blonde and silky. Her face is exposed, suddenly, completely. A warm smile, edged with apprehension,

"Hello, Jack, long time no see."

And I say "Hello, Nicky."

Marley looks at me, then looks at her, and lets out a couple of none-too-friendly barks, then approaches, sniffs, and her hackles go down, her tail wags. Nicky says, "How about the three of us taking a walk while Fizz is putting Flo to bed?"

I imagine that my state of dumb-struck shock looks obvious, and alarming. Nicky says, "It's fine, Jack, don't look so worried. This is about sorting out old problems, not making new ones."

I say, "OK", and call upstairs, "Just taking Marls out for a walk." Fizz and Flo do a duet of, "OK, see you later."

And, without more ado, the three of us head off to the woods.

I close the door softly, and we step out into the night. Marley is on the lead, walking to heel and looking, repeatedly, at Nicky. I'm looking straight ahead. Mostly. But I can see her, clearly enough, from the corner of my eye. She's just as obviously and solidly there as everything else, but despite her evident substance, I'm aware of the inescapable truth that she can't be real because she's long and well and truly dead.

We turn left at the Beecliffe gates, walk for a couple of hundred yards beside the main road, then take the footpath which crosses the fields and leads up into the woods. We walk in silence. But as we enter the woods, Nicky takes hold of my arm, clasping the bit of exposed wrist between coat sleeve and my hand, which is thrust, deep and sullen in the pocket of my jeans. Her fingers feel soft and cool against my skin.

It's the second time in my life that she has initiated physical contact with me. And the feeling is exactly the same now as it was with that first touch. It's delicious, and irresistible. And it feels desperately dangerous. Perhaps she is aware of my tension, senses the turmoil. Her voice, soft as her fingertips, says, "It's OK, Jack. I've come to try to put your mind at rest, not to give you fresh grief." My reply is curt and cold. "You've already told me that. So, how exactly does a dead person re-write history? How are you going to do that, Nicky?"

She says, "Just by telling you the truth. I think that's why I've been given my voice back."

I wrench my hand free from her in a spiteful jerk, and stare at her with wretched hostility. In that moment, I welcome the flood of anger which fills me and takes up all the space where my guilt and grief might otherwise be.

Marley looks up at the pair of us. She furrows her brow, woofs a bit, wags her tail, appears a bit perplexed. Then she seems to settle, and sits down, leaning herself against Nicky's leg. The three of us are frozen for a while, motionless and silent. Eventually, with a small and hesitant voice, Nicky says, "I've been stuck, Jack, for all this time. Ever since the day of the accident. And yes, it really was an accident."

A long pause. Then she says, "Well OK, I know, it's true that I had been wanting to kill myself, before. I just wanted everything to stop. Thinking that was my best option. Only option. But the truth is that I really did change my mind. I'd already written the letter to you, the one that I was only going to send if you got in touch first. But then I thought, No, I'm not doing that. I'm going to see you face to face.

"I was on my way to see you when it happened. I was sure that, the moment we saw each other, everything would be OK. We'd hold each other tight, and that would be it. I thought for a moment I'd bring the letter, as a proof of all the stuff that'd gone through my head before. But then I thought 'who needs the letter anyway?' so I just left it in my bedroom, ran downstairs, no coat, no crash helmet. I was just mad, literally, mad to see you.

"I was no more than a couple of hundred yards from home. On the scooter. Not even going fast. Then that bloody cat came out of nowhere, and I swerved, and went headfirst into the wall."

I listened. And in the space of a minute, at most, the anger drained away leaving in its wake a black hole of numbness.

Nicky says, "It was one hell of a crash, but the point is, that wasn't the end. My body was smashed to bits, beyond repair, but I didn't actually feel dead, let alone gone. I was just stuck, in limbo, full up with all the thoughts and feelings which had filled me in that last instant. Stuck inside that kind of a dream where your feet can't move and your entire body is frozen to the spot and time itself comes to a juddering halt."

At this point, Marley lets out a long loud yawn, and then rubs her muzzle up and down against Nicky's shin.

For some reason, I'm absolutely captivated by this movement, and feel a surge of emotion welling up and connecting me with both of them – sensing that all three of us are sharing a moment of being alive, together, and knowing it.

I say, "Nicky, can you feel Marley's head against your leg, or are we just figments, just part of your dream?"

And she says, "That's exactly the point, Jack. I'm not stuck inside that nightmare any more. That's what I meant when I said that I've got my voice back, I can talk again. With people. I can hear what they say, and choose how to reply, and then say it, whatever, out loud. I feel like I've turned into a Houdini who's escaped from the box which used to be my coffin."

And I say, "Well, well," and then, "Wow." And then I tell her that, once upon a time, I was stuck inside a kind of a coffin too, when I used to be Jack-in-a-box.

But I didn't really want to get into that whole business. I was starting to feel anxious. How long had we been out? Would Fizz and Flo be worrying? And then, the obvious-as-soon-as-you'd-thought-of-it question: what was I supposed to do with Nicky? Invite her in, do the introductions to my wife and daughter?

I look at her. But before I can get a word out, she says. "You don't have to look so terrified, Jack. I'll walk with you as far as your front door, but I'm not coming in. Not possible. That's your life. And I'm not a part of it." And without waiting for a reply from me, she says, "Come on Marley," and sets off.

As I fall into step beside her, she asks me, "What did you think when you read my letter? You did get it, didn't you? I know that my brother posted it to you. I watched him do it. The day after my funeral. He'd been sitting in my bedroom, crying, pacing up and down, ranting like a mad man, and then he saw it on top of the dresser, and he picked it up, looked as if he was about to open it, seemed to change his mind and just ran, out of my room, out of the house, all the way to the post-box and dropped it in. And he said out loud, 'I don't know what you've written Nicks, but Jack deserves to see it. It'll be the last thing he ever gets from you.'"

I tell her: "Yes I did get it. In fact, I've still got it now, but I've never opened it. I got it on the same day that the story of your accident was in the local paper. I had your letter and the paper in my hand, both at the same time. I read the paper's main headline, which said that the cause of your accident was unknown, but the effect was the simple, unalterable fact that you were dead. And I thought to myself that nothing in the letter could possibly change the fact of your death, so what was the point of reading it?"

I paused. Nicky said nothing. She just looked at me. I couldn't meet her eyes, could only stare at the ground by me feet, and then I said in a barely audible whisper, "Well, actually that's only part of it. The truth is that I was scared stiff, terrified in case you'd said that you regretted the fact we'd ended up in bed together, or that the thought made you sick, or that you felt I was a mean, horrible bastard – just like Kev. I didn't dare to

248

take the risk of reading any stuff like that. Not then. Not since. Haven't had the guts to read it, but also never felt able or willing to throw it away, so it's just stayed, locked shut by my cowardice. Abandoned but not forgotten."

Nick says a long, sad, "Dear, oh dear." And then, "When you get home, and when you've got some time to yourself, read it, please."

It takes us another quarter of an hour to get home. We're walking in silence, hand-in-hand. I feel the warmth of her skin, feel her energy, her heartbeat, sense her spirit. Under the front porch, I search my pockets for the door key. She says, "Thank you, Jack, for helping me to break out of that limbo I've been stuck in for all these years. And I'm glad for you, that you've found a way out of those silent dungeons you used to lock yourself into.

"Read the letter, Jack, and when you finish it, just wish me a fond farewell and a happy new life."

And then she was gone.

I thought, now, really, gone for good.

39

Thursday evening, ten past seven, I'm sprawling on the sofa, half asleep in front of the box. I'm in a kind of day-dream, which starts off with me thinking back to my original interview at Beecliffe, when I first encountered Dr Aveyleigh and Ken Kaminsky. And I'm musing about the fact that I had liked, and felt comfortable with Ken right from the start, whereas my attitude towards Dr Aveyleigh had gone through a one-hundred-and-eighty degree transformation, from contemptuous loathing to a deep and genuine respect. In the middle of these musings, there's an unexpected knock on the door. Fizz goes to answer it. I hear her say, "Hi Ken, how are you?" He says, "Fine, thanks Fizz. How are you? Is Jack in?" And I say to myself, "Well, I'll be…"

I'm hauling myself upright as the pair of them come into the lounge. Ken and I exchange Hi's. I ask him, "Tea? Or something in a glass?" He says that he's not on call, confirms that I'm not either, and extracts a bottle of single malt from its tissue wrapping. He asks Fizz if she'd like to join us in some celebratory toasting. She says, "Maybe a bit later, but I'm going to leave you boys to it while I sort out the mountain of mess that's invaded my kitchen. You want ice, water, both?"

Ken shows the label. It's Laphroaig. We both say, "Neither, thanks." And Fizz says "Righty-oh." She pops into the kitchen, and then returns with a bowlful of cashews and a couple of glasses – nice ones, Waterford crystal, anniversary presents from us to us last year. Ken carefully pours a handsome glug into each glass. We clink them together, say, "Cheers," and I ask, "To what do I owe the pleasure?"

Still standing, he closes his eyes, takes a serious slug, rolls it around his mouth for a couple of seconds before swallowing, lets out a long, delighted "Mmm," then sits down in the armchair, crosses his legs, and with the look of a very happy man all over his face, says, "Well, Jack, therein lies the tale."

It seems to me that the omens look good. So, I take a modest sip, savouring the pungent, peaty smokiness, pick up Ted, who's lying face down in the corner of the sofa, and with him in one hand, glass in the other, sit, and say, "Go on then. Tell me. I'm all ears."

Ken takes another sip, slightly more restrained this time,

then puts the glass down on the coffee table. He helps himself to a large handful of cashews and pops them into his mouth. All in one go. Chews. Slowly. He's taking his time.

Well. I'm certainly curious, and eager to know what's afoot. But I'm certainly not going to rush or badger him. These days, we've become close and comfortable in each other's company, so it's easy to sit back and take it as it comes.

Eventually, he swallows the mouthful of cashews, looks briefly at the back of his right hand, then rubs the remnants of salt from palm and fingers, then looks directly at me and says:

"Well, Jack. You know I've been away for the last few days, but I haven't said, to anyone apart from the Good Doctor Aveyleigh, where I've been and what I've been up to."

I say that I'd just assumed that he and the family had been taking a break in their cottage in Witton-le-wear.

Ken says, "Ah yes, but not altogether so. In fact, we did stay there last weekend. And Paula and the kids and her mum are all still there.

"But, on Tuesday morning, I took the train from Durham down to London. I had a job interview in Greenwich. It lasted the whole day, and by the end of the afternoon, the panel were all giving me handshakes and warm smiles. But they said that Equal Opps precluded them from telling me anything there and then. They'd have to formally notify me in writing. Well, the letter came with the second post this afternoon. They've offered me the job. I am, now, the newly appointed Principal of the Cutty Sark Regional Resource Centre for Children and Young People. Which is quite a mouthful. And I think, probably, quite a job."

I say, "Jesus, congratulations." I stand up, transfer Ted, whom I'd been holding throughout, from right to left, so I could shake the new principal warmly by the hand.

I call out to Fizz, "You need to come in here and join us. And bring yourself a glass." She came straight in, and within a minute, it's all hugs and refills and chinks and cheers. And, for the following couple of hours, there's a long crescendo of excitement, in which Ken first gives general outlines, and then elaborates his vision for the future.

Quite early on in these proceedings, Ken says something which raises our interest from the vicarious to the seriously personal. He explained that his own appointment as Principal of the Resource Centre is the first and only one so far. He goes on to say that his initial task, as soon as he's officially in post, will be to head the interview panel to appoint his senior management team. He says this will comprise four positions. His own, plus Head Teacher, Head of Remand and Head of Assessment. He focuses on the last of the list. He says that this post-holder will have direct line-management responsibility for the Centre's secure unit. He says that the Centre's theoretical model for its work will be based on social learning theory, but beyond that, nothing is set in stone, so the way in which the assessment process is designed and delivered is, essentially, up for grabs.

He says he would like me to grab it.

I say I'm not sure what that means.

He tops up my glass. Again. Then says, slowly and carefully, "Jack, I am inviting – no, I am encouraging you to apply for the post of Head of Assessment and secure provision at the Resource Centre."

I say, "Oh, I see."

Fizz says she sees too.

I say that I feel honoured and flattered, and a bit overwhelmed, and at the moment, a bit pissed. And I say that I'll have to think about all this very carefully and very soberly. And immediately Fizz says, "No, Jack. That is not true. No thinking involved here. The truth is that you do not have to spend any time agonising and chewing this one over. The truth is that this kind of opportunity comes once in a lifetime, and you, of all people, could not possibly turn it down. Because you would not be able to live with yourself if you walked away from this one. And, believe me, if you couldn't live with yourself, I sure as hell will not be living with you either. Ken, a refill please."

Ken dutifully does three refills, draining the bottle. We go chink, and cheers. And Fizz and I, just in that exact moment, without a whiff of doubt, know that our lives have now changed, beyond the previous limits of our imaginations.

40

This is seriously weird. I'm sitting in the train, which I caught in Durham half an hour ago. I'm heading down to King's Cross, then over the river to the Royal Borough of Greenwich, for my interview with Ken Kaminsky and co. Inside my jacket pocket is the letter from Nicky – the one I've mentioned, the one I keep talking about. The one I talked about with Dr M, in our final session, just last week. The one that still remains unopened, unread. My plan is to read it as part of this trip. Opening the letter will give me closure. That's the theory.

But. I can't make my mind up. Should I read it on the way

there or the way back? I feel like I'm a bit touched. In the head. Slightly demented. A half-baked nut-case. Ideas cavorting round like drunks on a wet-iced dance floor.

Here's a bit of the mangled mess in my mind. I've just seen Nicky again. Recently, and impossibly, given her status of being well-and-truly-long-dead. And when I saw her, she was fully there and real. And reassuring. Full of, "Don't worry Jack, it's OK. Just read the letter, there's no need to be afraid." All of which fails to remove the fear but succeeds in adding to it a large shot of irresistible excitement. And I'm on the brink. All of a quiver. Saving the best bit till last, and still delaying the moment of biting into the icing with the cherry on top. Delaying delight. And, it's like a Christmas present which looks just fabulous, as long as it stays wrapped, but still holds the potential for the doom of disappointment.

And, it's like the letter from the hospital, with the results from the lab. tests, pronouncing their verdict and sentence, all of which will remain unreal just as long as the letter remains unread.

For the moment, Nicky's letter remains where it is. Safely sealed, inside jacket pocket, next to the heart. Trembling in time to my pulse.

I'm gazing absently out of the carriage window. It's getting dark. And the darker it gets, the less I see of out, the more I see of my own reflection.

My eyelids start to droop.

The carriage is warm and slightly stuffy; the seat's soft and comfortable. I sink into it. The rhythm and motion of the train are drawing me, irresistibly, into a kind of trance. I'm not asleep, but I do start to dream in vivid colour and with razor sharp clarity. I can see both my hands, resting, loosely clasped in my lap. I watch my left hand as it pulls my jacket open by the lapel. My right hand reaches into the pocket and takes out the letter.

And I see that Nicky is here, on the train, sitting opposite me. She takes the letter from me, saying, "Would you like me to read it to you, Jack?" I say, "Yes please Nicky. Go on. I'm ready now."

I watch her as she slides her index finger under the envelope's flap. She slits it open in one movement. She takes the letter out and places the envelope face-up on the table. Her handwriting, my name and address, are all splodged and blotchy, with only a few isolated patches which have stayed unstained by the tears which fell on it all that time ago. I'm sitting; watching Nicky, looking at her hands, and see they're slightly trembling, which makes the sheets of paper gently quiver. I'm also watching her face. Her eyes are hidden-downcast in their focus on the letter, and then they lift and meet mine. For a moment, we hold each other's gaze, before she looks back down, to focus on her words. She begins.

It probably took about three – maybe four minutes. She read every single word, in a voice which was cool and calm and clear. She offered no extra bits of explanation, no editing, not a single pause to check out how I was taking it.

What it boiled down to was fairly simple, really. After our night together, and the morning's eviction by my raging, grief-drenched Ma, and our parting from the bench on the green, Nicky had gone home with a throbbing head and a bashed-up heart. She felt bad that my Ma had called her a slut, and she felt a whole lot worse that I hadn't said a single word to defend her.

Not at the time, apparently not since. So she'd started to wonder if everything I'd said to her that night was a bunch of crap. She wondered if I had thought that all I needed to do was ply her with booze and then she'd shag anyone. She wondered if Kev and I were just the same in the way we thought about her, whether it was the same thing, what we'd both done to her.

All of that stuff took up the first page-and-a-half of the letter, but halfway down page two, the writing changed from blue ink to black. The tone changed too. She said she didn't want to believe that Kev and I both thought about her in the same way. She wanted to believe that I really did care about her. And care for her. She thought that she might feel safe with me – protected by me. She wanted to be with me. But she felt frightened to tell me all, or any of this stuff, in case the truth was that I didn't give a toss about her. So, she made a deal with herself. She was going to write down all her feelings as clearly as she could, but she was not going to send the letter. Not until she'd heard from me. And she was giving me one month. If I hadn't got in touch with her by the end of September, then the letter would be ripped in pieces and dumped in the bin.

All of that stuff took the letter down almost to the bottom of page three, where it ended, saying,

> *I just hope so much, that you do get in touch with me, Jack.*
> *I hope that you'll give me the courage, and the reason to send*
> *this letter to you."*

> *Nicky*

And then, right at the bottom of the page,

P.S. It's been on my mind, nonstop, for weeks now, a constant preoccupation. Is it real, or am I just imagining it? Well, now I know, for sure. It is real. You're going to be a Daddy, Jack.

That is the end. She folds the letter, replaces it in the envelope, tucks the flap in, and hands it back to me.

Then I just sit there, gazing at her.

In that moment, the only thought in my mind is how absolutely, unbelievably gorgeous she is. And as I'm gazing at her, it's as if, for the very first time, I can, genuinely, see her. Recognise her existence. Realise her presence. Know that I know her. Love her, completely, body and soul.

I close my eyes, and feel time slipping away, trickling through my clenched fingers, sentencing the present to the past.

41

We'd been busy packing for the whole day, so by eight in the evening Fizz and I agreed, enough's enough, the last few bits could wait till the morning. We were in the kitchen, and Fizz asked, "Where's Flo"? I said I didn't know and went upstairs to look. The bedroom doors were all open, revealing bare floorboards and a forlorn emptiness inside. Only the bathroom door was shut. Muffled sounds were escaping onto the landing – bits of whispering along with the odd "shush". I stood outside, trying to eavesdrop, dithered for a moment, then knocked and asked, "You OK in there Flo"? A brief pause was followed by, "Yes Daddy.

We're all in here and we're all fine. You can come in if you like". I said that I would like, opened the door and went in.

Flo was sitting, fully clothed, inside the empty bath. She was holding Ted in one hand and her polka-dot-bikini doll in the other. Marley was also in the bath, sitting to attention at the opposite end from Flo and somehow managing to look both alert and sheepish at the same time.

Flo said, "I've been talking to them about you, and I've told them that you seem to think that I'm not really able to talk for myself, so you end up putting your words into my mouth." She paused while Ted whispered something urgently into her ear. She reacted, at first with a stern look, though this gradually softened into a smile and then she said, "Oh alright then. That's what you used to do, but hardly at all now".

I asked her if she thought this change was for the good, and she said, "Definitely," while Ted and bikini-doll nodded in vigorous agreement. I asked how come they were all in an empty bath together and Flo explained that it was the only place in the whole house that didn't feel empty and sad. She asked me if I wanted to join them but I declined, saying that the bath looked pretty full and anyway I wasn't sure if they'd finished talking. Flo said that she did have more to say, but it was OK for me to listen if I wanted to because now nobody had to keep any secrets. I thought to myself, "Yep, thanks be to God that's true", but all I said was, "You lot can have another ten minutes in the bath, and then its bed-time and I'm going to tuck you all in for the very last time in this house." Then I hauled myself to my feet and walked onto the landing, feeling like a very large lump of suspended animation with a throbbing head and an aching back. I could barely move, so I just lay down where I was, stretched out full length on the bare boards, cradling my poor head in the crook of my arm. Meanwhile, a few feet away the bath-tub conversation resumed.

The great big sticking plaster seemed to be getting a lot of attention. Flo was saying, "That plaster used to be huge and stained and nasty looking. But the worst thing about it was its smell. Really awful. Like a lot of disinfectant trying to hide something rotten." She carried on, but more quietly and for a while I couldn't make out a word. Then, the volume went back up. "And now that its nearly disappeared I think that I know what it used to be for. I think that Daddy needed the plaster to keep all his hurt feelings inside of him. To stop them from spilling out and making a stinky mess." Then Flo started quoting some of my own words, saying that I had started to realise – at long last – that it was worse than useless trying to lock these feelings inside because they would find a way to escape, and then anyone in range could catch bits of upset as if they were the measles, at which point I butted in, saying, "That bit really is true, I'm sure of it". And Flo said, "Yes, Daddy. We all know now".

Everything stopped for a moment. Then Flo cleared her throat and said, "Only one bit left now. What Dr M said to me. I've remembered every word, as if it was a poem I'd learned by heart. She said:

"'Sometimes we don't really understand our feelings until we start trying to put them into words. We can say the words out loud, and as we say them, we can hear them too. We can listen to our words and then decide whether or not we agree with what we've said. And the best thing of all is, after we've spoken, and listened we can, if we choose to, decide to change our mind'. That's what Dr M said, and that's what we've done, both of us, me and Daddy, we've decided to change our minds."

I'm lying down and feel like I'm glued to the spot, stuck in the no-man's-landing. But the head and back ache have both gone, disappeared like melted snowflakes. And very gradually, I begin to realise that it's not just me here. Of course, Flo and Co are all still in the bath, but apart from them, I've got company.

First of all Nancy is here. She's hiding behind the bathroom door, both hands held up in front of her face, peeping through her fingers then jumping out and yelling, "Boo," at Flo. Both of them erupt in shrieks of pretend horror and howls of absolute delight.

My Dad is here too. He's clearly loving the twins' mad antics and then slowly looks away from them, looks straight at me and says, "Come here, Jack. Time for a hug." We hold each other. He's warm and solid and he smells of polished shoes and a whiff of pipe smoke.

The brand-new baby is here as well. She hasn't grown a proper body yet but is starting off with nothing more than a real peach of a smile.

In fact, it looks like absolutely everybody is here, and they've all got the same, simple message. They're saying to me, "It's alright Jack. You can relax now. We've all come to tell you. You're not on your own kid".

42

It's a warm day, blessed with a gentle breeze, which sends the wisps of white fluffy cloud gliding across the spring– cleaned sky.

Marley has been anxious all morning, clearly unsettled by the whole process of us taking the boxes and beds and bits and bobs out of the house and into the enormous van. Now, the house is empty. And full. Of echoes. But Marls has just seen her travel-rug go into the back of the car, and little Flo has said to her, "Don't be a silly dog, of course you're coming with us." And somehow, the old pooch seems able to accept these words as a total antidote to all her worry.

Now, Marley is sitting quite still on the lawn, sniffing the air. Fizz comes out of the door, walks sedately up the path and manoeuvres herself into the front passenger seat of the car. She winds the window down, leans her head out and says, quite formally, "Listen, house, I am not saying good riddance. I am saying goodbye, and thank you. Thank you for keeping us all safe and sound here. And thank you for providing us with the perfect place to create the beginning of a brand-new life. Bye-bye, house." And with that, she winds up the window and stretches the seat-belt over her voluptuous boobs and blossoming belly.

Marley takes this as the "prepare for lift off" signal, and makes a headlong dash, jumping in through the open tailgate and onto her blanket. I slam down the hatch, checking to make sure it's locked tight.

We've already finished the whole "goodbye" routine. We pleaded with everyone not to hang around to wave us off, but to let us go, quietly, by ourselves, when we were ready.

We're ready now.

In this precise moment, everything in my mind, in fact, everything in the whole world, feels beautifully balanced and poised. We're on the brink. Me with a new job, all of us with a new home to move into and a new life to live. It feels like we've been granted the miracle of a fresh start with a clean slate. All in all, life, hope and spring seem as if they're about to start bursting out all over.

I feel an itch. It demands my immediate attention. And action. My hand moves irresistibly towards my belly. My great big mitt fumbles, then manages to undo a couple of shirt buttons, then slides inside, scratching luxuriously around the source of the itch. The skin is soft and tender to the touch. The skin has a mind of its own. It recognises the texture of my palm, fingers and nails. It breathes in deeply. Then pauses, motionless and timeless, before breathing out in a long-overdue sigh of quaking relief.

The hand homes in to the exact centre. Nothing of the plaster now remains. There is no residue. No remnant, just a tiny bit of fluff, which I take between thumb and forefinger, and raise to arm's length above my head, then release, and watch as it floats away on a warm breath of wind.

Acknowledgements

Before it became a book, *Alright Now* existed as an evolving manuscript which was passed around various friends and family. Their responses were warmly encouraging and gave me the impetus to keep going along the path to publication, so my thanks to them all. Without their support, Jack Warren would never have emerged into the wider world. As well as this nurturing group, I would like to acknowledge the specific contributions of two people. Firstly, my wife Malka, whose faith in and encouragement of me as a writer has been steadfast throughout the (almost) fifty years of our marriage. Secondly, I am indebted to my friend Peter Furtado, who has enthusiastically undertaken the roles of editor, advisor and gentle nudger – all of which were needed to transform the disparate bits of the book into a viable prospect. Lastly, I would like to thank my former colleagues and all of the kids in care with whom I worked and from whom I learned so much throughout my career.

For more information about the origins and evolution of *Alright Now*, please visit my website www.geoffwarr.uk.

Further Information

Many TV programmes – particularly those with highly charged emotional content – end with a message saying, "If you have been affected by this programme, you can find further information/help/support by visiting..." I wish to make a similar offer to anyone who is reading or has read *Alright Now*. The book explores some seriously tough issues, including sudden bereavements, traumas and their aftermath, mental health problems and the use of drugs, both in their prescription and recreational or self-medicating forms. All of these matters are addressed in greater detail on my website www.geoffwarr.uk.

As a shortcut, here are some websites that may be helpful:
- Bereavement: cruse.org.uk (This offers help in your local area, learning more about grief and access to online one-to-one support from grief counsellors.)
- Counselling services (local provision): emotionalmatters. co.uk/counselling/services

References

Within the book, there are a number of references to professionals who have worked in the fields of psychotherapy and child psychoanalysis, foremost among whom are Melanie Klein and W.R. Bion.

For more detailed information please visit my website where you will also find pointers to a much wider range of psychology textbooks, papers and novels which have all contributed to my thinking on the subject of emotional development in general and extreme events in particular.

The music of The Incredible String Band plays a significant role in the book, as it has in my life. Lyrics from 'October Song' are quoted in the context of a child's funeral. In fact, the quotation is not entirely accurate as it conflates lines from different verses but that's how Jack misremembers it, and it's how he always sings it. Please allow him this slight leeway.

Lightning Source UK Ltd.
Milton Keynes UK
UKHW012231120721
387051UK00001B/61